JEFFERS(

DNA

A Novel

by

Reid Eikner

Dedication

For Diane

Acknowledgment

The author would like to thank several people who helped make this book possible:

Dr. William H. Snell, RADM US Navy Ret., for his help in forensic dentistry.

Robert K. Perry, for his book and expertise on ground penetrating radar used in cemeteries.

Elizabeth A. E. Dodson for her help as a first reader and editor.

Sandra L. Eikner for her help in domain name registration and website designer.

About the Author

Reid Eikner is a native of Charlottesville, VA, and a graduate of the University of Virginia's School of Engineering and Applied Science. He also holds degrees in business and law and had a 37-year career in business in various executive positions. He is a military veteran of the U.S. Army Corps of Engineers including service in Vietnam. He is retired and lives in St. Johns, FL, with his wife of 51 years. In retirement, he taught as an Adjunct Professor in the Business Minor program at the University of Virginia's engineering school. He has lectured frequently on Jefferson in the Florida area, including seminars for the OLLI affiliate at the University of North Florida.

Chapter One

When his cell phone began to vibrate on the bedside table, Dave Hutchinson did not recognize its muted ring because he was having some good REM sleep in his new retirement house outside of Charlottesville, Virginia. He had purchased an existing home in the Bellair subdivision on the west side of town with the proceeds of the sale of his longtime home in New Jersey across the river from Philadelphia. He particularly liked the new home because it had lined bedroom drapes to keep the room interior dark until sunlight broke through each morning, and it was near one of his favorite lunch spots, an Exxon gas station that had remodeled its mechanic's bays into a thriving sandwich shop. Besides, the phone's vibration buzzing reminded him of the quarter-fed vibrating beds in the early 1980s in countless motels on the East Coast he had slept in during his career at Comcast Corporation as a field project manager. But the constant buzzing finally brought him to the realization that he needed to answer the annoying phone. When he picked it up, the lighted dial showed the call was from Charlie "Chuck" Conrad, his field supervisor on a special job they both had taken on in retirement.

"Hello, Chuck. What is it?" Dave said in his best sleep monotone.

"Sorry to bother you so early, Dave, but I think we are getting close to the cross-over point. The core drilling samples last night showed a sharp increase in wood fiber in the soil, most of its white oak. Tonight's sample showed a lot of wood fibers on the screening level, even more than last night's screening did." Chuck responded to his boss.

"What time is it now, Chuck?"

"Five thirty am, but it looks like a beautiful Virginia spring morning," Chuck said, trying to put a positive spin on the matter,

1

"the birds are up already and talking to each other, and there is a pale light of pre-dawn in the eastern sky."

"OK, go ahead and shut down the drilling for tonight, secure the property and get some sleep. Have the night security guards stay on patrol around the project perimeter until the day security team arrives at 7 am. I will contact the property owner later this morning to see if he wants to be present when we start back drilling later. If he wants to be here, it will mean a night off for the drilling crew and then drill again on Thursday night."

"Right, will do. You know how to reach me and the crew later today. Good night or good morning as the case may be."

"Thanks, Chuck," Dave said as he put the phone back on the bedside table.

He lay there for a while but realized that it was futile to try to go back to sleep. Besides, for over 30 years, he was used to getting up at this time because, in construction work, projects started around 7 am unless you were working in residential areas, then you got a break and delayed starting until 8 am. Dave was born and raised in Albemarle County and graduated from the University of Virginia School of Engineering and Applied Sciences in 1982 with a degree in Civil Engineering. Right after graduation, he was able to land a field project manager job with Comcast Holdings (the name of the company at that time) because he had two summer internships with them while still in school. He also had correctly expected that any engineering or business employer would want him to become a certified project manager as soon as reasonably possible after employment. So, he began to take some of the course work to become a certified project manager associate supplied by the Project Management Institute (PMI) in his last year at school. His professors were disappointed in his lack of interest in becoming a PE (professional engineer), but Dave was an outdoors guy and not at all interested in design work or research. He had achieved the required 36 months of project management experience by the end of his third year at Comcast and had taken and passed the rigorous Project Management Professional (PMP) certification six months later.

Dave traveled a lot during his first five years at Comcast, and it was great fun at first. In the 1980s, Comcast embarked on an ambitious investment program of installing fiber optic cable throughout its East Coast footprint toward becoming the dominant internet and cable television provider in its market. Dave became a major part of the actual installation teams sent out every week from the Comcast headquarters in Philadelphia, but the travel part of his job wore on him, especially during year seven, which he attributed to the "seven-year itch" when employees begin to think their career was stalled and some change was needed, even if it meant changing employers. But Dave had been assured that the travel part of his job would not last much longer because his manager was retiring soon, and he was the heir apparent to become Vice-President of Project Management for Comcast. Unfortunately, Dave's boss didn't have many hobbies other than work, and he lingered on the job before retiring in 2000. One of Dave's crew foremen during those years was Chuck Conrad.

Chuck had started out in Texas in oil drilling in 1978 at the age of 20, but that industry had moved to drilling mainly off-shore wells in the Gulf of Mexico and into the heartland of Alaska near the Arctic circle, neither of which were at the top of Chuck's desired location list. He was born and raised in the coal mining area of western Pennsylvania and was an all-state lineman in football in high school. But he attended a small high school of just under 800 students and played, therefore, in one of the "lower-rated" high school leagues in the State. Also, he was undersized for college football at only six feet and 210 pounds, even though his heart was the right size. So, Chuck roamed the Midwest for a couple of years after high school picking up labor jobs requiring strength until he landed a job as a roughneck for an oil drilling company in Houston, Texas. In 1984, he decided to return to his Pennsylvania roots and was able to get a construction crew job with Comcast late that year. Six years later, he was a crew supervisor, and his men liked his tough

3

but fair managerial style. Dave liked his engineering problem-solving skills even though Chuck was not an engineer by education. Over time the two men became good work friends who respected each other's talents, but they didn't let that carry over into too much social interaction outside of work. Each of them had different interests; Dave played golf and read a lot, and Chuck drank a lot but never let it be to excess in frequency or amount or to the point of affecting his performance on the job.

Dave had married Marsha Freeman in 1989, but the marriage was strained from the start by the amount of time he was away overnight on Comcast projects. Marsha was two years behind Dave at Albemarle County High School, and they were casual friends in high school because Dave played sports and dated a classmate and friend of Marsha's until his high school graduation.

After graduating from high school, Marsha went to Mary Washington College in Fredericksburg, VA, for two years but left college to be with a marine she met at a school mixer. He was stationed in nearby Quantico, VA, but a year later was deployed to Parris Island, SC as an instructor, and she never heard from him again. She worked for a while as a waitress in Charlottesville and then moved to Philadelphia, where an uncle helped her get into a teller training program in 1986 at Philadelphia National Bank. She happened to see Dave in her bank one day two years later and reintroduced herself to him. They dated for six months and then decided to get married as they both were ready to settle down supposedly. Dave had agreed that Marsha would not have to work once the children were born. Unfortunately, Marsha's first pregnancy two years later resulted in an ectopic pregnancy, and the child had to be aborted along with losing one ovary. Marsha had a hard time shaking that post-event depression, and the physical and mental turmoil it created made another pregnancy too difficult for both of them. After two years of joint marital counseling, they agreed to no-fault divorce in early 1994 and went their separate ways.

Dave gave Marsha one-half of the net sales proceeds of their modest starter house and agreed to fund two years of college for her should she decide to pursue a degree, but she never did nor asked for more help. A few years after the divorce, Dave heard she was living at the New Jersey shore and working in a gift shop at the beach. Dave bought another small two-bedroom home in a different New Jersey suburb of Philadelphia and began to improve it with a rear deck facing a lake and finishing off the basement into a TV and entertainment area, plus a workshop. He had a regular lawn service since he was away a great deal of the time.

Dave had some romantic interests, even after 2000, when he became Vice President of Comcast and traveled out of town less often. But by then, he was over 40 and seemed content with his bachelor life and golf at Pine Valley, one of the most exclusive, private, and demanding courses in the country. Becoming a member at Pine Valley took five years of careful planning and meeting the right people at the right time. Dave didn't particularly like that part of the process, but the golf course was something special, and the owner-members had a right to be picky since it was their money behind it all. After 38 years, he retired from Comcast in 2020 during the height of the Covid pandemic because he didn't like working from home, and he thought it was time to let go. He was 60 years old, and the company had an attractive early retirement bonus plan for employees who were over 60 with 30 years of seniority. Dave moved to Charlottesville in the summer of 2021 and joined Farmington Country Club that fall for the golf season of 2022.

Dave's phone went off again, and he hadn't realized that he had fallen back asleep. It was now seven-thirty. So much for getting up and getting going like he had earlier thought he would do. He didn't recognize the phone number that was shown on the phone face, but it had a local area code and might be a golf friend from Farmington. He decided to risk it and answer the call.

"Hello."

"Mr. Hutchinson?" The caller asked. That was the first sign of possible trouble, but Dave was stuck now and not thinking clearly after his renewed REM sleep.

"Yes."

"Mr. Hutchinson, my name is Sam Carpenter, and I'm a reporter for The Daily Progress newspaper here in town. I'm sorry to call you so early, but I have been trying to reach you for several weeks about some questions I have about some work being done...."

"Click" – Dave ended the call and quickly proceeded to block any further calls from that number. He made a mental note to try to figure out who or where the reporter might have heard about his current project and especially how he got Dave's cell phone number.

Dave showered, and while he was doing that, his mind was racing with possible ways his cell phone number could have been obtained by the local press. He used "burner" pre-paid phones for calls to his crew members and to rent the blue tenting material used on site along with the equipment. And he had non-disclosure agreements with both the equipment lessor and tenting lessor that had penalty payment clauses if the disclosure was traced to them. Surely none of the drilling employees would have said anything; they were all hand-picked by Dave and Chuck and had signed confidentiality and non-disclosure agreements. Besides, they were living together in a hotel, almost in a sequestered arrangement with burner cell phones of their own. Their bonus pay for success was sizable and was withheld until the project results could be publicly announced. And surely no one from the property owner's staff would have tipped off anyone.

Then it hit him; he wondered if this was the same young man who was caught snooping around the project work site right after the drilling had just started or maybe it was the guy who had come over to his table at Timberlake's Drug Store café last December and said he worked for the *Daily Progress*. If it was the latter, then he must have hacked into somebody's cell phone because there were no

6

introductions made in that encounter. Maybe someone hacked into the property owner's cell phone calls and then began to make random calls. Dave and the property owner's representative were visible around town and had lunch once a month in the early part of the project, but now they hadn't had lunch since drilling started earlier this month. The "maybe" game always infuriated Dave. He dealt with known facts, problems, and solutions, and this world of subterfuge, secrecy, and dishonesty didn't sit well with him. But this project required all of them, and then some, and Dave wanted it to be completed successfully so that, afterward, he could travel again in the world of the known.

While shaving, Dave continued to let his mind race down the train track for a possible breakdown in the privacy of his project. For years, Charlottesville has had an NSA phone monitoring facility on the north side of town. Could the press have bribed someone there for a phone trace? There was already an earlier problem with an NSA Special Agent. It was starting to worry Dave about whether the project would have to be shut down right when it was getting close to a defining moment.

After dressing, Dave sat down with another "burner" cell phone and texted the property owner's representative, as he had mentioned he would do in his early morning call with Chuck. It had been six weeks since their last lunch in January.

The message said, "It's Dave. It's Plan Jefferson for Friday at 12 noon." Both of them had decided on a code as to location, date, and time. Location was done by a former President's name, which would mean the President's number was equal to the same letter number. Since Jefferson was the third President and the third letter was C, it meant the location name started with a C. The lunch meeting would be at the Chick-fil-A restaurant in Barracks Road Shopping Center. Other locations they had used in the past were the Adams Plan which meant the lunch meeting would be at the Bellair Market at the Exxon station on US 250 W, but they had not used that location at all because it was not private and too close to Dave's home. A similar plan for Chester Arthur, the 21st President, meant that the lunch meeting would be at Timberlake's Drug Store in their long-standing café in the back of the pharmacy where Dave had many a lunch during his childhood and school days in Charlottesville. It was a staple of downtown Charlottesville for generations but was used only once to meet there as a last-minute substitute last August to settle on a bonus payment plan for the project workers. It has not been used at all since then because the venue is small and not very private. The Quincey Plan meant the lunch was at Farmington Country Club. It had been used frequently last year but not used since last month because there was only one way in and one way out of the Farmington property and no guard shack to stop unwelcome visitors. A visual stake out could be made easily at the property entrance, and any party to the lunch could be followed afterward. In fact, that had already happened twice, most recently in January. The date was always one day before the date in the text, and the time was always set at 1.5 hours after the time indicated, so the lunch would be at Chick-fil-A on Thursday at one-thirty pm.

Dave used his personal cell phone to call Richard Dunleavy, a long-time friend whose family had lived next door to Dave's family while growing up in Albemarle County and who had retired back to the Charlottesville area just last year like Dave had done. Nine months ago, at the beginning of the project, he and Richard had purchased a used pickup truck in Richmond and titled it in the name of a fake company that had its own bank account set up by Dave for the project. The pickup truck was parked at Richard's apartment complex on the south side of town near Monticello High School. The apartment had several individual buildings with numbered parking spaces for a car for each unit and then additional unnumbered spaces for guests, second cars, etc. The truck was parked two buildings away in one of its unnumbered spaces. Both friends had keys to the pickup truck and to Dave's personal car, a medium-sized silver Chevy SUV.

When Dave first approached Richard about this arrangement, he said he couldn't explain the reasons for the truck or its private and confidential purpose, but when the project was ready to go public, Richard would be the first to know the results. And the bottom line was that Richard could keep the truck for his participation if things went south and the project failed or was canceled. But Richard was now working for the project as part of the day security team, so the pickup truck was useful, along with his presence at the work site. Dave knew that Richard was off today and tomorrow after working over the weekend.

"Hey there, brother, how are you?" Richard said when he saw who was calling him. Richard had a career in the marines and called every good friend "brother." He had attended the University of Richmond for two years and then left to join the marines. He stayed in the marines for 30 years and served in both the Desert Storm and Iraqi Freedom campaigns. He was wounded in each conflict and now had a nice government pension for his long-time military service and free VA benefits for medical care until he died. He enjoyed landscaping and decided to settle in Charleston, South Carolina, because there were plenty of jobs for landscapers in the low country and a good VA hospital was nearby. After ten years there, he decided to return to his roots and moved back to Charlottesville in early 2021. He spent his time after returning to Charlottesville involved in outside activities which focused on helping others, such as being a volunteer at the Martha Jefferson Hospital on Pantops Mountain. This was typical for Richard as a lifelong "giver," and he wanted to "give something back to the community" for his gentle, quiet, and loving coming-of-age time in his life.

"Rich, I'm good. I need to use the pickup truck today for a couple of hours. Can I get it from the normal place near your apartment, or were you planning on using it yourself?"

"I was not planning on using it, so it will be here," replied Richard, "But I am heading to the new Center at Belvedere this morning, so I can park it there if that will be better."

"Actually, that does work better for me, so do that, and you can use my car for your other needs later," said Dave.

"Sure, what time is good for you?"

"Eleven-thirty works for me if that fits your schedule," Dave said.

"Ok, that is fine with me, see you then, semper fi," and Richard hung up. The usual place was the Charlottesville regional senior center on the north side of town until the project drilling started earlier this month. The new senior center was called the Center at Belvedere, and they decided to drop the name "Senior" because it was not just for old people. Anyone over 50 could become a member. Richard would park the pickup truck in the back of the center and wait for Dave inside.

Dave left his house at ten o'clock that February morning and drove onto the old Charlottesville By-Pass, built around 1955 through town without any notion or space for expanding the number of lanes from two each way, which was fine 65 years ago, but entirely too crowded now. He headed east toward town but immediately turned off at the Barracks Road exit to stop and look at men's pants at Eljo's, a fine men's clothing store on Millmont Street. Eljo's had been the clothier of male students at the University of Virginia for over 70 years, but with the addition of female students in 1969, the male student dress code tradition of wearing a coat and tie to class began to lose its appeal. By the late 1970s, when Dave attended the University, coats and ties were optional and only worn by a minority of the male students. Even the faculty had begun to ditch the coat-and-tie professional appearance for college teaching, but Eljo's had clung to the classic male clothing look and countered its loss of sales volume with increased pricing and more branded clothing with the Virginia colors of navy blue and orange and more clothing with the Virginia sports logo. Besides, Eljo's was locally owned, and Dave was a loyal purchaser from his student days through to the present day, only less frequently until returning to Charlottesville two years ago. Two pairs of pants and sixty-five minutes later, a conversation with the owner and his son about what's wrong with students and people today, Dave left Eljo's to drive to the Center at Belvedere, about 7 minutes away on the north side of town.

As Dave pulled into the front of the Center's parking lot, he looked into his rear-view mirror to note any cars that pulled in with him or were lingering on the street at the entrance driveway. Seeing none which looked suspicious, he turned the engine off, removed the keys, and stepped out. He waited a few minutes to see again if there was anything unusual about the car traffic outside the center. He then closed the front door to his SUV, locked it with his key fob, and went inside.

Richard was sitting at a 1000-piece picture puzzle game table with two chairs in the center's main activity room. He stood up as he saw Dave approach, and they both shook hands and added the male partial hug, right shoulder to right shoulder.

"Good to see you, brother! How is everything today?" said Richard, as he did his usual two-hand-squeeze handshake as a token of long-term friendship.

"Just fine, Rich. How is the VA treating your war wounds?" Dave would always counter, "and are you getting up more than once a night to pee?" Which was a common joke between them about getting older.

"Have you got time to talk?" Rich asked, hoping that Dave would sit for a spell like most senior citizens did at their age. Although the activity center had other seniors there, they were at the fireplace sofa setting or out of ear range. Besides, some of them didn't hear so well anyway.

"I've got 30 minutes to spare; anything urgent on your mind?" Dave responded, thinking Rich might have something that was troubling him.

"Nothing that I can't handle with the VA in Richmond, but that's not why I asked. I thought I saw the *Daily Progress* guy following me when I left the project site yesterday. From our earlier intervention with him this month after drilling had just started, I know he drives a blue Volkswagen Jetta."

"Yeah, he's been tailing me a couple of times recently but not stopping me or interfering yet. He's like a Birddog on a hunt right now, but he doesn't know how to hunt or point."

Richard continued, "By the way, I was hoping we might make another trip to Hilton Head to see the Heritage Golf Tournament again, maybe next year. I know you like to plan ahead, so if that is of interest, I'm in also."

Richard was referring to a trip they had taken to a rental house on one of the fairways on the Harbour Town Golf Course, where the annual RBC Heritage Golf Tournament was played. They went with two other Charlottesville friends in 2016 after doing something similar to Augusta National Golf Club for the Masters in 2013, except that the rental house definitely was not on the Club grounds. Those trips had been the last golf trips Dave had taken after all the money he had spent on golf in his lifetime. But for old retired guys, taking trips or sitting around a fire and talking about past good times and the stories they generated was like a tonic for the soul. After another 25 minutes of "remember when" stories, Dave decided it was time to wrap this visit up with Richard.

"Another Hilton Head trip would be fun someday, but I can't focus on future plans until our project is completed," Dave said the last word with some emphasis to indicate to Richard that he really needed to get going.

"Let's plan dinner next week on one of your days off, Rich. You pick the date and place. I will come by your apartment later today to exchange the truck for my car."

"Sounds good. I will call you this weekend with the date and place. Vivace Restaurant still has great veal piccata."

"Just text me, if you don't mind, I think someone may be trying to hack into my phone, and it might be our *Daily Progress* guy," Dave replied as he got up and then went out the back door.

He unlocked the door to the pickup truck and started the engine. Everything looked normal, except the gas gauge showed a need for gas, which was understandable due to the lack of use of the truck and the high cost of gas in 2023. He looked into the rear-view mirror for a while as he pulled around to the front of the senior center and exited the facility. How the heck did he get involved in this cat-and-mouse game in retirement in July of 2022, he thought as he pulled onto the northbound lanes of US 29 even though he wanted to go southbound actually.

Chapter Two

Mid-July 2022

It was the middle of July 2022 when Dave Hutchinson first got the telephone call from Roger Pettit, a lawyer friend of his and a member at Farmington Country Club like Dave. Roger was a classmate of Dave's in 1982 at the University of Virginia and had stayed on grounds to attend and then graduate from the Law School. After passing the Virginia bar exam, Roger stayed in town as a new associate attorney in the medium-sized law firm of McGill, Summers & Smith. About fifteen years later, he and Virgil Brown began to slowly buy out those senior partners, and eventually, they became the two senior partners in Pettit & Brown, PA, one of the largest law firms in Charlottesville. In that telephone call, Roger had asked if Dave could meet him for lunch at Farmington the next day.

At that lunch, Roger explained that he represented a group of property owners whose association name would remain anonymous for this first meeting. They and their association had been clients of his firm for many years and had asked his help in finding and engaging an experienced project manager for an extremely important and difficult project requiring utmost secrecy until the results of the investigation had been determined. Any further details would have to await a later meeting, but everyone involved in the project would be expected to sign confidentiality and non-disclosure agreements. The pay part of the project would be in two parts; one for undertaking it, which would be at a high weekly salary for each person involved according to skill level, and a second one for a successful result, a bonus payment, so to speak, equal to 25% of the sum of all the weekly salary payments each person worked to protect the privacy of the project, and that part would be withheld until a public announcement of the results of the project was made or until the association determined not to make the findings public. In either case, a successful and undetected project result would trigger the payments by a special Swiss bank account along with all the weekly salary checks. The project timetable was expected to be completed in about nine months, including time on the client's own property.

"This whole thing sounds fishy to me and possibly against the law," Dave said after Roger had paused long enough for Dave to get a question into the monolog.

"I can personally assure you that it is completely above board legally, and there will be no payment reneging or delays," Roger said emphatically. "This is the first of several lunches we will have to allow me to explain more of the project to you. Time is of the essence. But Dave, you need to think about this proposal and give me an answer at our next lunch meeting two days from now. Are you free to have lunch here again then?"

"Yes, I'm free."

"Good. If you agree to head up the project and agree to sign your confidentiality and non-disclosure agreement at our next luncheon, the sum of $15,000 will be deposited into your checking account from a private Swiss bank account before the next business day. You and all project workers will be considered independent contractors and be responsible for paying your own FICA and income taxes. Here is a draft of your confidentiality and non-disclosure agreement for you to look over before our next luncheon. If you are in, bring your bank account information with you next time so we will have the correct wire information."

Dave thought for a few seconds and said, "Is there anything else you can tell me now about the project?"

"Only this," replied Roger, "you will be expected to set up another bank account in the name of a fictitious company you make up and then make an initial deposit of $10,000 into that company's own bank account from the first $15,000 you will receive after our next lunch meeting. This company account should have a minimum number of checks to pay for project expenses, plus Zelle privileges to wire money for payments if a vendor prefers that form of payment. Any amounts paid by you from that account will be

15

reimbursed to you the following week after filing a detailed statement with me. If you accept this offer, give me a name you want to use for this company, and I will set up an LLC for you and a friend whom you can trust to be the other officer. Also, you will need to set up a post office box at the US Post Office on US 29 North and let me know the box number. That will be the mailing address for the fake company. The company will be involved in gravestone restoration work if that will help you decide on a name."

"You will be free to leave the project at any time before the project is completed, but any future weekly salary payments to you of $5,000 will be cut off immediately, and the conditional bonus will become null and void. You will be expected to honor your confidentiality and non-disclosure agreement or face a possible lawsuit later. This is not a threat, just a reminder of the seriousness behind this project and its importance to my clients."

"Thanks for the reminder, Roger, and I will see you here in a couple of days," Dave said as they both stood up to leave and shook hands. "I have a lot to think about before our next luncheon." Dave went down to the Farmington golf shop to browse through the new golf drivers in stock. He wasn't sure why he felt uncomfortable and needed to avoid leaving with Roger at the same time, but everything about this luncheon was unusual.

Dave wasn't sure about the project or his role in it, but the $5000 per week would be nice to build a ready cash account for future travel or some other emergency. Two days later, at the next luncheon meeting with Roger Pettit, Dave signed his confidentiality and non-disclosure agreement and gave it back to Roger, who seemed very pleased with this result. And then Dave said,

"Use the name Virginia Stone Restoration Company, LLC (VSRC) as the name of the company. Also, use Richard Dunleavy as the second officer, but only my name is needed as a signature on checks as President and Treasurer. I went by the Post Office yesterday and opened up a box in the name of VSRC, and its address is PO Box 1245, and the zip is 22903."

Roger said, "Great. I will take care of all that and give you the paperwork to take to your bank for setting up the company account. This project requires the utmost secrecy to be successful, and you should expect the press and others to want to find out what is going on at the project site. You should get some pre-paid cell phones to use for calling anyone, and you will need a first-class supervisor who doesn't mind working at night and who has experience with a Ditch Witch horizontal drilling machine. You will also need ground-penetrating radar equipment and maybe GPS equipment. All this equipment needs to work in a difficult environment with extreme precision required. You will need a drilling work crew of a sufficient number of people as you determine later, and they also need to be used to working at night because there will be no drilling or work on-site during the day."

"Where is the property, Roger? And why all this secrecy?" Dave asked after a slight pause.

"I can't tell you that right now, but I will be able to tell you soon. For the entire two months on the owner's property, a security force of 2-3 armed guards for both day and night shifts will be needed with strict no-trespassing regulations in place. Finally, you will need to hide the work with tenting canvas; maybe 8-10 feet high will be needed to shield the work from outsiders. Some parts of the property need to be left visible to preserve the property's value as a tourist destination."

"So, what is the next step, now, Roger?" Dave asked, hoping to get some real substance and direction from his friend.

Roger responded, "Your next assignment is to look into some tentative vendors for all this equipment, manpower, supplies, and a potential crew supervisor. At a later date, each vendor contracted will need to sign formal non-disclosure agreements in exchange for premium rentals. Once you have that preliminary data on hand and a crew supervisor in mind, give me a call, and we will meet for lunch here again. I will then have more information for you about the dates and timing of the project. Have a good day, and welcome aboard."

"Thanks, I think," Dave said in return.

After the second luncheon with Roger Pettit, the next day, $15,000 showed up deposited into Dave's bank account from an international wire transfer, so he picked up the legal documents from Roger and went to his bank set up a separate checking account at his bank in the name of Virginia Stone Restoration Company, LLC (VSRC), the fake company. He opened that account with $10,000 from his own bank account and ordered company checks which had the company name and post office address. He then went to Walmart to buy ten pre-paid phones for his "ten employees" of VSRC to stay in touch with each other during the work day. He used one of them to call the HR Director at Comcast to see if she would give him a contact phone number for Charlie Conrad, who had recently retired. She wasn't there the first time he called, so he left a message. Fortunately, she called back the next day with the requested information, so he didn't have to have a long discussion about why he wanted to contact Chuck in the first place. Dave then broke up that phone with a hammer and put the pieces into separate trash bundles to put out for pickup on different days. He kept the SIM card and put it into the last bundle of trash to put it out the following week. He looked up Ditch Witch online and found there was an authorized dealer in Glen Allen, Virginia, just northwest of Richmond, not too far from Short Pump, Virginia. Dave also located three tent vendors in the Charlottesville area, most of them to the east and south of town. He also found four security firms in the Charlottesville area that appeared to have people for the project, but he wasn't sure that any of them would have people with the "right" stuff. And he bought a used pickup truck and titled it in the name of VSRC. He intended to have Richard become the owner of the pickup truck after the project was completed as a way of thanking him for his trusted name, military service, and his friendship over many years. The expenses to date were turned in to Roger, and replacement funds were wired to the VSRC bank account for the project in due course.

One week after the second luncheon with Roger Pettit, Dave was ready with some early information for him. Another $5000 from the same international wire transfer had been deposited into his personal bank account by the time he and Roger met for a third lunch at Farmington. Dave reported the early information on Ditch Witch dealers, tent suppliers, and security providers in the Charlottesville area. He also said he left a message with his old friend and crew chief at Comcast. But Chuck had not called him back yet. Dave felt it was time to hear what this project was really about, so he asked Roger point-blank,

"What kind of project is this work, and who is the property owner, Roger?"

Roger paused for a moment and then said, "You have done well so far, Dave, and here is the rest of the story," mimicking the words of the radio broadcaster Paul Harvey.

Chapter Three

Roger Pettit was the same age as Dave Hutchinson but had become used to a career centered on a desk or table. He was showing signs of joint stiffness in his normal walking gait and could stand to lose about 20 pounds. But he had that "trust me" countenance on his face, topped by grey to silver hair and lots of it still. And he knew people, both in Charlottesville and in Richmond. After placing their lunch order for their third lunch at Farmington, Roger asked Dave,

"Do you remember hearing about the DNA study done in 1998 to try to determine if Thomas Jefferson fathered one or more of the children born to one of his female slaves, Sally Hemings?"

Dave answered, "I remember some of it, but not all the details. I know there was some problem with the people sampled because Jefferson did not have any male heirs. And I think there were some issues about how the results were interpreted."

"The DNA study was fraught with mistakes and issues, and the interpretation of the results by the study personnel, headed up by a retired pathologist named Dr. Eugene Foster, was over the top compared to the actual scientific results. The publication of those interpretations in a British scientific journal spawned two additional studies, one by the Thomas Jefferson Foundation, which owns and operates Monticello, and the other by my client, the Monticello Association, which owns the Jefferson cemetery area adjacent to, but separate from, Monticello. The work done by the Thomas Jefferson Foundation is on their website, and copies of it are in this binder you can take with you. I have also put in that binder copies of a later rebuttal of the Foundation's work actually done by the Thomas Jefferson Heritage Society, a new entity that has a similar membership to my client. Rather than me summarizing these efforts, I will let you read the materials on hand, and you can form your own conclusions. I will be interested in your conclusions at our next luncheon when I will tell you more about what has occurred since then to put into motion the current project my client wants you to complete for them."

"Thank you for all this copying and background information," Dave said as their lunch food arrived.

For most of the next two days, following receipt of the background information from Roger Pettit, Dave read and re-read the materials supplied to him. He summarized the information in handwriting on three sheets of paper, one for the DNA study, one for the Foundation's study, and one for the Society's study. After he completed the first two summaries, he got a return call from Chuck Conrad on the burner phone Dave had used to call Chuck in the first place, so he hit "accept" the call button and said,

"This is Dave. If you're calling to speak to a doctor, press one; if you are calling with a complaint about an unpaid bill, press two; if you are calling about a female companion for the evening, press three." Dave and Chuck had used this routine in phone calls before, so Dave knew that Chuck would not interrupt or get confused.

"This is Chuck, and I don't have a digital phone to press a number. How are you, old man?"

"Who you calling old," Dave bantered back, "You pre-date the dinosaurs and lived before there was fire, but how are *you*, old friend?"

"Not bad for being older than dirt. I would have called earlier, but I was deep-sea fishing off the coast of New Jersey until a couple of days ago, so I didn't get to hear your call until yesterday. And this is a different cell phone number than the one I remember."

"Wow, sounds like quite a trip. How was the fishing?"

"Got some tuna but not much else, and I got sick as a dog which surprised the hell out of me since I never had that problem before. The ocean was really rough and choppy, with some waves at 15 feet. And no one had any Dramamine. What's new with you and the new house and new phone?"

"I'm good, and the house is a work in progress, but it has good bones. I had it repainted inside before I moved in to get rid of the all-white hospital approach of the previous owners. I now have three bedrooms rather than two like in New Jersey, so I decided to make the extra bedroom into a man cave with a very large TV and all my office stuff. I don't know why I thought that would be important at the time, but it has been very useful lately. The phone is new for a reason."

"So, other than a nice chit-chat about old times, you mentioned a possible business opportunity in your call. What's that all about?"

"I have been engaged as an independent contractor for a project involving Ditch Witch horizontal drilling equipment, ground penetrating radar, GPS location accuracy, secrecy, foreign espionage, and women spies."

Chuck laughed out loud and said, "you are still embellishing the story and understating the difficulties."

"Got me again. I was wondering if you could drive down here and stay with me for a couple of days, and I will fill you in on the problem and the solution. I can't talk about it on the phone, and that's the reason I'm using this burner phone. In fact, I will destroy this phone after our conversation is finished."

"I have a couple of things on my calendar for tomorrow, but I can be there mid-day on Thursday," Chuck said after coughing a couple of times.

"I hope you haven't been exposed to Covid, but Thursday will be fine. As you come into Charlottesville on US 29, you will cross over the Rivanna River, and there is a Walmart on your right shortly after that. Go into their parking lot and text me on my regular cell phone that you are here, and I will drive out to meet you. You can follow me the rest of the way to my place. Looking forward to seeing you. Are you still drinking Maker's Mark?"

"Same here, and yes on Maker's Mark, but less of it than before due to doctor's orders. I will text you Thursday from Walmart," and Chuck hung up, which was normal for him since he wasn't much of a phone person. He preferred direct one-on-one communication, which made him a good field supervisor.

Dave broke that burner phone into pieces like its' predecessor and discarded the pieces in a similar fashion. He then completed the third hand-written summary, which was the client's rebuttal study. He decided that Friday would be a good day to meet Roger for lunch with Chuck in town. Maybe that would be enough to convince Chuck to join up if he had any reservations after hearing about the project on Thursday. He used another burner cell phone to call Roger and set up the fourth Farmington luncheon for Friday at 1 pm.

Shortly after 3 pm on Thursday, Dave's personal cell phone lit up with a text message,

"I'm here,"

Dave texted back,

"I'll be there in 20, park in the area of the lot closest to the main road."

As Dave turned left off of US 29 north at the Walmart light, he looked into his rearview mirror by habit now to see the traffic turning with him. He again turned left into the Walmart parking lot, and rather than going straight back toward the main highway, he went down the entire length of the parking area first. Several cars behind him pulled into earlier aisles, so eventually, no one was behind him. Then he turned into the last aisle and went all the way back toward the highway. He saw a car with the driver's window down and a door partially open and saw Chuck inside, so he eased his car in front of Chuck's car and signaled for him to follow him, which Chuck did.

When they got to Dave's house in Bellair, they shook hands, and Dave asked Chuck if he needed any help with bags. Chuck traveled light and said no, he could handle everything. After showing Chuck to the guest bedroom, Dave said he would go fix some drinks. It was too hot outside to sit on the screened-in porch even with the fan running, so they settled into comfortable leather chairs in the living room, Dave said,

"Great to see you and have you here. Thanks for coming all this way."

"Likewise, for me, so what's this project all about?" Chuck said, not wanting to mince words, as usual; he had a way of getting right to the matter regardless of the subject.

"I first need you to look over this VSRC confidentiality and non-disclosure agreement and see if you have any problems signing it."

"Wow, really clandestine stuff, Mr. Hutchinson. Sounds interesting and maybe illegal. And who or what is VSRC?" replied Chuck with a grin.

"VSRC is for Virginia Stone Restoration Company, LLC, the company I set up for this project. And everything is very legal and legitimate, but the client is super sensitive to secrecy. So, are you willing to trust me on this one?"

"Give me a few minutes to look this document over." After a few additional seconds, Chuck said, "OK, I'm in as far as signing the document and trusting you." He signed the form.

"Well, that was fast. I appreciate your trust in me, old friend." Dave said as he smiled. "OK, here are three summary pages I have developed that will be the easiest way to catch you up with what I know. Look these over while I fix us another drink."

"Make mine just a half, I'm supposed to cut back on this stuff, and I had a long drive which makes me want another one even more," said Chuck frowning all the time.

Dave went into the kitchen, and Chuck began reading the three sheets of paper Dave had given him. He was facing the front window, which looked out onto the street in front of Dave's house. The second time he looked up, he saw a large black SUV drive by slowly one way in. The side windows were tinted so Chuck couldn't see the driver or if there was more than one occupant in the car. As he finished reading the third paper, the black SUV slowly drove back out the other way, picked up speed, and drove off toward the entrance to the Bellair subdivision.

When Dave came back with the drinks, Chuck said, "are you aware that someone in a large black SUV might be casing your house for some reason?"

"Not at all. When did you see that, just now?" said Dave as he put the drinks down and moved up to the front window.

"Yeah, it came by slowly and then sped off," answered Chuck, "it might not be anything, but my gut tells me you need to be careful."

Dave sat back down and said, "There is a lot a secrecy surrounding this project, and it appears someone wants in on it who isn't on the approved need-to-know basis."

Dave then summarized his three sheets of paper, starting with the DNA study first.

"It appears that in 1998 a DNA study was undertaken to determine if Thomas Jefferson was the father of one or more children of a female slave by the name of Sally Hemings. This study seems to have been the brainchild of a retired pathologist by the name of Dr. Eugene Foster, who was working part-time at the University of Virginia Hospital. There is no indication that Foster had been engaged by any other party, such as the Thomas Jefferson Foundation, owner and operator of Monticello, Jefferson's home. Blood samples were taken with prior permission from (1) a current male descendant of Eston Hemings, the sixth child and last son of Sally Hemings, (2) three current male descendants of the Carr brothers who were Jefferson's nephews and lived full-time at Monticello with their widowed mother, a sister of Jefferson's, (3) five current male descendants of a Thomas Woodson who claimed that Woodson was the first son of Sally Hemings whom they believe was pregnant when she returned from Paris with Jefferson in 1789, and (4) five current male descendants of Field Jefferson, an uncle of Thomas Jefferson since Jefferson had no direct male heirs himself."

"Foster had wanted his study to be underwritten by the American magazine *Science*, but they declined. He was able to get the British scientific journal *Nature* to support the study, provided his DNA samples were analyzed in England. There were a couple of problems with the Foster study procedures ranging from minor to major. First, he did not split the blood samples so that a future independent study might have to use the same samples to confirm the original results. And second, he carried the samples overseas on a plane to England, which raises certain questions regarding the chain of custody issues and refrigeration. The Foster results were typical for male paternity issues then, meaning that they could be helpful in eliminating specific males from paternity, but their flaw was they could not be conclusive as to including specific males as fathers unless there was a direct male heir and the sample tested."

"The study concluded that there was no paternity relationship between any Jefferson descendant and any Woodson descendant, thus eliminating any Jefferson from being the father of Thomas Woodson. That fact destroyed the Woodson family's oral history retold over eight generations. There was no paternity relationship between the Carr descendants and Eston Hemings descendants, thus eliminating the Carr brothers from being the father of Eston Hemings only. The study was not structured to see if the Carr brothers fathered any other child of Sally Hemings because there were no other Hemings male samples to test against, even though there were male descendants of Madison Hemings, the fifth child of Sally Hemings and older brother of Eston Hemings, up until 1940 when the last grandson of Madison Hemings died. The Madison Hemings family had denied access to that gravesite for a possible DNA sample. Finally, there was a paternity relationship between the descendants of Field Jefferson and the descendant of Eston Hemings, thus indicating that SOME Jefferson fathered Eston Hemings, but it was not conclusive that it was Thomas Jefferson himself."

"How does DNA produce all these results?" Chuck asked.

"Good question," said Dave, "I'm not a doctor, but I think the key is the male Y chromosome. It passes down through generations of males in the same family almost unchanged, so the chemical structure can be identified and thus be connected to specific males."

"OK, so what was the outcome of this DNA study when it came out in the British journal?" asked Chuck.

"Without any further scientific proof other than the father of Eston Hemings was A JEFFERSON, Foster concluded that was enough evidence to say that Thomas Jefferson was indeed the father of Eston Hemings. And he stated that conclusion in his published journal article, which he authored along with several other European doctors, none of whom were Board certified in the US. It was certainly an unscientific and headline-grabbing conclusion for any professional to make. It was almost like Dr. Foster wanted this conclusion to be the outcome all along. Like any breaking news today, this November 1998 report was a bomb shell in the US, and news people here wanted to know what the response of the Thomas Jefferson Foundation would be."

"I assume this brings us to the second summary sheet," said Chuck.

"Very perceptive of you," said Dave in a deadpan voice, "The Foundation indicated it would immediately form a study committee to review the available information on the DNA study and provide its conclusion at a later date. By December 1998, the Foundation had formed an internal-only staff Committee to review the findings of Foster's DNA study and make its own conclusions concerning the possible paternity of Thomas Jefferson as the father of one or more of the children of Sally Hemings. This Committee had at least two Foundation members, including the Committee chair, who had published books and articles previously about the importance of oral histories of Jefferson's slave families in understanding the slave

28

culture and life at Monticello. They and several authors believed that oral histories of slave families had been discounted in previous investigations of the possible Jefferson paternity issue, so they were biased toward giving these oral histories more weight even though they lacked scientific proof. The Committee only had one medical doctor, who was added as an assistant interpreter for the Committee."

"From the timing of various report drafts, it appears that the Committee had come to its final conclusions very quickly, by early March 1999, in fact, after only three months of discussion, yet their official report was not released until January 2000, a delay of another nine months. The Committee also had a dissenting opinion which was authored by the one medical doctor on the Committee, but his dissenting opinion was not discussed in a Committee meeting or even distributed to the other Committee members before the release of the Committee's final report to the public. As expected, the Committee gave great value to the oral histories of the Hemings family, especially to the families of brothers Madison and Eston Hemings. It also used Jefferson's own notes in various Farm Books to establish his presence at Monticello at loosely calculated conception times for all the children of Sally Hemings, even though Jefferson's notes were not recorded every day, nor were they specific as to his whereabouts once he reached Monticello. The Committee's conclusions published in 2000 used qualifying words like "likely" and "high probability" in assigning possible paternity directly to Thomas Jefferson himself. By 2018, those qualifying words were eliminated from the Foundation's records even though no new scientific evidence had been added to the volume of materials on this issue."

"So even though there was no direct scientific evidence beyond the DNA connection of one son of Sally Hemings to SOME

JEFFERSON, the case against Thomas Jefferson said he was guilty of fathering ALL of her children," Chuck said in a summary fashion.

"Yep, that pretty well sums it up," Dave added as he picked up the third piece of paper. "Our client is the Monticello Association, which owns the Jefferson family graveyard adjacent to, but separate from, Monticello itself. The graveyard was purchased in 1913 by a group of lineal descendants of Thomas Jefferson from the owners of Monticello at that time, the Levy family. Some ten years later, the Levy family sold Monticello to the Thomas Jefferson Foundation to put Monticello into a public trust for future generations to see and enjoy this remarkable house of an American patriot and founder."

"Turning now to the third sheet of paper, another study was published in the fall of 2002 by a newly formed entity named the Thomas Jefferson Heritage Society, which featured its own committee of 13 experts who worked on the available Jefferson materials for over a year. That committee's report found by a 12 to 1 vote that the DNA study and the Foundation's work were biased against Thomas Jefferson and that the case for his paternity of six children of Sally Hemings was far from proven. Therefore, since 2002, the Association has maintained the position that only lineal descendants of Thomas Jefferson, with proper genealogical proof, may be members of the Association and thus have burial rights in the Jefferson family graveyard. The Association recognizes that its membership is dependent upon documentary genealogical evidence, which is generally unavailable to descendants of slaves, but other evidence is not fool proof either, as shown in the DNA rebuttal of the Thomas Woodson family's oral history."

"What a story and interesting triangle of people and events," offered Chuck as a way to conclude what seemed like a tutorial to him. "I'm ready for another drink and then dinner out if that is OK with you."

30

"Sounds like a plan," said Dave, "and by the way, we have lunch tomorrow with the Association's attorney, a friend of mine whom you should meet. I'm surprised you haven't asked about the salary involved in this endeavor."

"I figured you would tell me when it was necessary," replied Chuck.

"$3000 a week is your salary, but you pay your own taxes and your own expenses when you need to be here on a full-time basis. You are welcome to stay here on a sporadic visit basis, but I know you like your own space, so when it becomes necessary to be here all the time, you can handle that yourself or the project will provide housing for all the out-of-town contractors."

"Now, how about that dinner," said Chuck, "Is there a good Italian place you would recommend?"

"I know just the place," replied Dave, "and I will drive." The two men left and headed to Vivace's Restaurant, Dave's favorite Italian place.

The next day, both Dave and Chuck arrived at Farmington Country Club around 1 pm for the scheduled luncheon with Roger Pettit, the Association's attorney. The Grill host said that Mr. Pettit had called to say he would be a little late because he was picking up someone at the airport and would see you about 1:30. So, Dave and Chuck went out onto the back patio of the Farmington Grill and sat down and both ordered iced tea. They proceeded to watch several groups tee off at the first golf hole on the Farmington course, and Dave commented on the various flaws in each person's swing, like the TV announcer he wanted to be in his second life.

Around 1:45 pm, Roger Pettit arrived with another person whom he introduced as Jonathan Coolidge, who happened to fly into town that day for some other business. Roger felt it was a good time to introduce him to Dave, who he expected would be alone. Dave immediately got out Chuck's signed confidentiality and non-disclosure agreement and handed it to Roger to put aside any issue that may have been created without it.

"Dave and Chuck, I want you to meet Jon Coolidge, who is the current president of the Monticello Association," Roger said, "let's go inside where it will be quieter, and we can order lunch."

After sitting and ordering lunch, Roger said, "Jon is a direct lineal descendant of Thomas Jefferson's granddaughter Ellen Randolph Coolidge. Jon, I had already briefed you by phone on Dave's background, and now he has his first hire in Chuck, so progress is being made toward the project. Why don't you brief them about how the project came to life within the approval process of the Association?"

"Sure," Jon started quietly, "for the last 20 years since the DNA study publication, the Foundation's report release, and the Jefferson Heritage report, the Association has had to consider an application for membership by a descendant of Sally Hemings nearly every year. Those requests have been turned down at our annual meetings in May of each year in spite of serious disagreements within the Association's current membership. After our May 2018 annual meeting, the Foundation held its own July 4th celebration at Monticello. At that event, they welcomed into the Jefferson family all the descendants of Sally Hemings present. It then removed the previous qualifying language from its 2000 report and changed its website to show without a doubt that Thomas Jefferson fathered all six of Sally Hemings's children. By the Association's next annual meeting in 2019, we had five descendants of Sally Hemings applying for membership in the Association and a strong indication that one or more of them expected to the buried in the Jefferson family graveyard when they died. The Association denied those applications, and our continued denial of these applications for membership had made the Hemings descendants angrier each year to the point where in 2021, we had one individual picketing our May annual meeting luncheon at the Omni Hotel. This past May was the worst, as the picketing had grown larger in number and volume. One of the members who are highly in favor of allowing into memberships, the descendants of Sally Hemings, is also very wealthy. He indicated in our annual meeting in May that he was willing to fund a way to get DNA directly from Thomas Jefferson himself."

The table got very quiet at that point, probably because their food had arrived but also because of the gravity of Jon's last statement. After the wait staff had departed and they were once again alone, Jon continued,

"Our annual meeting then erupted into loud shouts of disapproval at that point because many in our group thought it meant the exhumation of Jefferson's grave, starting with the removal of the obelisk grave marker over his coffin. But the member in question said that should not be needed. He explained that DNA could be obtained from the teeth of a deceased person even thousands of years after their death, as has been done recently with an Egyptian mummy using the FBI's DNA laboratory for analysis. And he was willing to put his money where his mouth was, provided the Association was equally willing to follow the science if the science showed that Jefferson indeed fathered Eston Hemings. The Association voted to look into this possibility, underwritten by this anonymous member, to settle scientifically once and for all time the paternity question about Thomas Jefferson."

You could have heard a pin drop at the lunch table. Then Chuck suddenly realized the significance of Jon's explanation. He gasped and said,

"You mean we are going to drill into Jefferson's grave from the outside to be near enough to his head to get a tooth DNA sample? Oh, my God."

"My sentiments exactly," said Dave, almost choking on his lunch, "And you want us to figure out a way to do that without any major disturbance to his skeleton or gravesite?"

"Well, not exactly." said Jon, "First of all, Jefferson's remains are surrounded by family members on all four sides, and there is no way our Association would allow any disturbance of any kind to his gravesite."

"But Jefferson had a younger brother by the name of Randolph Jefferson. Randolph was 12 years younger than Thomas Jefferson and had a twin sister named Anna Scott Jefferson. They were the last two children of Peter and Jane Jefferson. Randolph Jefferson inherited from his father an estate called Snowden in the Scottsville area in 1776, and he fought in the Virginia militia under Colonel Thomas Nelson in the Revolutionary War. He married his first cousin Anne Jefferson Lewis in 1781, and they had five sons and one daughter, but his wife died around 1798, and he remained a widower for the next ten years."

"Eston Hemings was the son of Sally Hemings, most like Jefferson according to oral histories in terms of height, while his brother Madison was much shorter, which may or may not be significant. Randolph Jefferson lived only fifteen miles away from Monticello during his time as a widower and was known to socialize with the slave population when visiting Monticello, playing the fiddle and dancing half the night away, as one oral history put it.

After the DNA controversy arose, historians began to take sides, and some of them thought Randolph Jefferson was a more likely candidate to be the father of Eston Hemings, who was conceived around late August 1807. There was a letter invitation from Thomas Jefferson to his brother to come to Monticello around that August conception time to visit with their sister Anna Jefferson Marks because she and her family were moving west, much further away. There is no record as to whether Randolph actually came to Monticello or did not come, which has left a void that perhaps now can be filled. Two of Randolph's oldest sons were in their twenties and old enough to father children also. Ironically, the oldest son was named Thomas Jefferson, Jr. and was 25 at the time of Eston Heming's conception. Both of these sons visited Monticello even more often than Randolph Jefferson."

"Randolph Jefferson remarried in 1808. He died in 1815, some 11 years earlier than his brother Thomas, and was buried at Snowden. But two months later, the entire Snowden estate burned to the ground and his widow, Mitchie Pryor Jefferson, left the now-vacant property to return to her family's roots in Buckingham County further south. The Snowden property then became tied up in a legal battle between Randolph's sons from his first marriage and his second wife, who was an absent widow. It was a battle of two Wills, meaning which one was the latest and authentic, and Thomas Jefferson himself provided a copy of the first one, dated in 1808, written in the handwriting of Randolph Jefferson prior to his second marriage. Thomas Jefferson later completed a deposition for the court as to its authenticity. That Will stated that the Snowden property was to be sold and the proceeds divided among Randolph's five sons. The second one was dated 1815, when Randolph was very sick, and it favored his second wife. Mitchie Pryor Jefferson was considerably younger than her husband. She had accumulated a lot of debts in his name to the point that local Scottsville merchants required his signature on her purchases which sometimes meant his signature was forged by her. So, Randolph finally adopted a special mark to authenticate her purchases approved by him near the end of this life, and this second Will did not have that special mark attached to it, and that Will was ruled invalid by the court."

"When Thomas Jefferson realized that a third party was going to own Snowden, we believe he decided to have Randolph and his first wife's remains disinterred from Snowden and brought to Monticello for burial in the family graveyard. This belief is based on a Jefferson letter written in late 1815 to his sister, Anna Jefferson Marks. We believe further that Randolph's remains are in the front Southwest corner of the cemetery to the left of Jefferson and his immediate family, but little is known about the alignment of Randolph's body or the condition of his wood coffin. Jefferson may not have gotten stone grave markers done if he believed that one of Randolph's sons wanted to have the coffins of his parents moved at a later date. Even if there was a stone marker at some later time, it disappeared before the graveyard was purchased by the Association in 1913. In the DNA world, it won't matter whether the unmarked grave is Randolph Jefferson's or one of his sons, but all the supporting evidence seems to point to Randolph rather than one of his sons being in that Southwest corner."

"What an amazing coincidence," said Chuck, "So why wasn't Randolph's remains considered for a DNA sample back when that study was first released?"

"Several reasons," Jon continued, "First of all, no one connected with the Association had any knowledge about the Foster 1998 DNA study prior to its release, nor was there any contact from Foster for information on this possible additional Jefferson grave. Second, once we heard about it, there was little scientific knowledge about bone marrow or tooth pulp from a deceased person being a source of DNA material. Third, you have to remember that in the early

1990s, even DNA testing of blood or organ tissue was in its infancy. Only after about 1995 did those sources become scientifically acceptable as the norm for DNA studies for paternity cases. Only in the last ten years has the science of dental DNA become standardized. And finally, we are not absolutely sure that there are human remains in that Southwest corner and, if there are, whether they are Randolph's or not."

"Why not just have a normal exhumation now of Randolph Jefferson's skeleton for a DNA sample?" Dave asked.

"That is a possible back up plan, but the Association believes that every burial in our cemetery in the past and in the future is special and disturbing any one grave needs to be avoided. Some graves are sacred, but all of them are special. In addition, the Association wanted this project to remain as secret as possible until we knew the DNA result. So, we want to find out if there are human remains in that Southwest corner and if it's possible to achieve a DNA sample in a less invasive way than exhumation. This is where you come into the picture. The anonymous association member has placed $1 million in a Swiss bank account and given Roger here authority to release wired funds for this project."

"It seems to me," Dave offered, "that the project is three-fold, first to determine if, and it's a big if, there are human remains in that Southwest corner and is a way to access those remains without exhumation, then second, is the skeleton in a position to retrieve a tooth sample sufficient for a DNA test. If all of that is a go, then the third fold is getting the sample itself as the final part of the project. After that comes the key element for your association, which is some laboratory tests and comparison to past DNA analyses."

"That's a good summary," said Roger, "And parts two and three will require finding a forensic dentist with the skill and tools to get that DNA sample, and I have some thoughts on that when you get past part one. As the Association's legal representative, we can't have any of this work be done sloppily or have the scientific result become invalid due to poor-quality procedures or samples, or not generate a large enough sample to be split and saved for a second confirming test if that becomes an issue. Jon will be in town once a month for the next six months to hear updates directly from you and allow us to evaluate your progress. He has the authority to proceed further or cut the project off if we determine that the risk is too great or if secrecy has been compromised to the point of making the project a public embarrassment. If there is any inquiry made about your work, you are to say it's in preparation for routine maintenance and remark some of the older gravestones, some of which have weathered badly over the last 200 years, but nothing is being done to Thomas Jefferson's grave or gravestone."

"Is it possible to gain entrance to the cemetery area, say on Monday, when there might be fewer people around compared to this weekend?" asked Dave.

"Yes," said Roger, "I have brought a key to the side entrance lock," he said, handing the key to Dave. "There is a gate on the west side about 20 feet up from the Southwest corner where Randolph Jefferson's remains might be buried. Make sure you don't lose this key and give it back to me if you leave the project or when the project is completed one way or another. Here is some history on the origins of the graveyard and how the Association came to be the owner of that property. It is essentially what is on the Association's website," and he handed Dave a packet of printed material.

Chuck said, "Do either of you mind if we need to put some surveying benchmark nails in place for later use? They definitely will be small and not readily conspicuous."

"Don't overdo it, and don't make it obvious that some work is going to be done within the graveyard," replied Jon, "Roger, can you

38

call the attorney for the Foundation and request one 'vehicle pass' in Dave's name to allow him to bring a vehicle onto the roadway leading to the graveyard? Tell them it's a contractor looking to bid on a possible repointing of the lettering for some of the gravestones there, but the work will not involve Jefferson or his immediate family under the stone obelisk, nor will the view to his gravesite be blocked from tourists. We will contact them again before any work is actually done and outline our plan when we know the extent of the work that is needed."

"Dave, access to the graveyard is very limited, and it is through the Foundation's property, so we have to be respectful of their rights and concerns about the impact on the tourist trade, which brings in a large amount of revenue for the Foundation each year, something approaching $8 million in annual ticket sales, especially since they were closed to the public for so much of the last two years due to Covid."

Roger said, "I will call Harrison Battle at Battle and McGuire in Richmond and see if I can get a favor done. They really don't like other traffic on those narrow roads around the home since they use their own bus system to ferry people from the visitor center to the home and to the graveyard. If Battle allows it, the pass will be at the visitor center for you to pick up Dave. I will text you if there is a problem or if it needs to be picked up from some other location."

"OK, let's hope this works because access to the site is damn important to this project," said Dave, "By the way, is there any reason why a large black SUV might be trying to check me or my house out? We had a suspicious car drive by yesterday."

"Not that I am aware of," said Roger, "has that car or anyone in it disrupted you by making you stop or talking to you or making any harassing phone calls?"

"Not yet," said Dave.

"If that tailing does happen again, try to get any information on the car if you can, and let me know," Roger said. "I will check it out. By the way, let me know Chuck's bank information, so I can wire his salary to him. And let me know when you have something new on the project to convey. We can have another lunch then. At that time, I want to discuss a videography plan with you before any work actually gets underway."

Chapter Four

Mid-August, 2022

On the drive back to Dave's house following the "explosive" luncheon at Farmington, the two men were quiet for a while, apparently lost in their own thoughts about the project.

"Well, you have certainly bitten off a chunk of dynamite this time, Mr. Hutchinson," said Chuck as they turned into Dave's driveway.

"You got that right, Chuck," said Dave, "I should have seen it coming. The signs were all there, I just didn't connect the dots." He stopped short as he saw through his car's rear view mirror a large black SUV slowly drive by his house, headed toward the Bellair entrance as though it had been stationed further down the road waiting for someone to come to his house. Dave immediately put his car into park, jumped out, and ran up to the street. He tried to get a look at the rear license plate, but the vehicle was too far away, and the plate did not look familiar; it was certainly not a standard Virginia plate in color.

"Damn, what the hell is going on?" Dave asked Chuck as he came back to his car and moved it all the way down his driveway. "There is something else happening besides a little grave robbing here. I couldn't see the license plate, but it was different." The two men went into Dave's house and sat down on the leather couch in his living room.

Then Dave continued, "Let's divide and conquer on the weekend work before going to the cemetery on Monday. Chuck, why don't you check online at Lowe's or Walmart or wherever to see about renting a portable GPS backpack? I will do the same for a ground-penetrating radar unit. I guess the best thing is to rent them for the day on Monday and then decide whether or not to actually buy one or both for future use."

"You haven't been in the field lately, have you, Dave?" said Chuck with a smile. "Every Comcast field office has that equipment today to locate underground utilities and make accurate measurements for repairs or new property development installations. Let me make some calls to see where the nearest location is which has that equipment is. Maybe we can borrow a set for a day."

"Great, yes, it's been a long time since my field work days. Here is a burner cell phone to use for making your calls. I will line up a pickup truck for Monday, and we need to go to Target to get some more burner cell phones."

Chuck went into the guest bedroom to get his book of phone numbers and make some calls, so Dave used his regular cell phone to call his marine friend Richard Dunleavy.

"Hey, there you are, brother. How's it going?" said Richard after seeing who was calling.

"All good here, Rich. I wanted to see about using the pickup truck for the day on Monday. I need to haul some gear and do some work on my project." Dave answered.

"It's here and can be picked up, or do you want to meet somewhere so you can get it from a staging area? I was planning on going to the new Center at Belvedere off of Rio Road on the north side of town Monday morning for an exercise class and then a morning history talk."

"The Center would be ideal and park the truck in the back. My car will be in the front when you need to leave later."

"That will work for me. By the way, guess who came by the hospital yesterday while I was there working."

"The President, they want you to run the Parris Island marine training camp?" Dave said with a smile.

"Nice try, no, it was Lucy Carlisle. You remember Lucy. She was in town visiting her mother in the hospital. Her mother had a stroke but is expected to get out of the hospital next week. Lucy asked about you, and I told her you recently moved back to Charlottesville and that we get together from time to time. She asked me if I had any contact information for you, and I told her to give me her number, and I would pass it onto you the next time I saw you."

"Of course, I remember Lucy," said Dave, "we dated in high school, and she was a friend of Marsha's at school. I haven't seen or heard anything about her for 40 years. As you know, I didn't come to any of our own class reunions, and Marsha never went back for any of hers either."

"She looks terrific," Richard offered, "and apparently, she is a recent widow who lives in Richmond. Her husband died of Covid in 2020, and she was very sick from it also but recovered. Do you want her number?"

"You hold onto it for now; I will think about it and let you know after the project is over. I wouldn't even know what to say to her after all these years, and I need to focus on the project."

"What do I tell her if I see her at the hospital again when her mother is discharged? Work doesn't always have to come first, does it?"

"No, but right now, I have too many things going on to think about a social life involving new or old females. Just tell her I have a current project that keeps me busy from seeing any of our old friends at present. I'll see you around 9 am on Monday, but I won't be able to talk long at the senior center." Dave said and then hung up.

Lucy Carlisle, Dave thought, imagine that. His musings were interrupted five minutes later when Chuck emerged from the guest bedroom and reported,

"Success! There is a Comcast field office in some place called Short Pump, which is…."

"I know where Short Pump is," interrupted Dave wanting to speed up this process.

"Anyway, I have the address, and I talked to the Superintendent there. Turns out its still Chet McNamara, and he remembers us from 15 years ago and has agreed to lend us the equipment we need for the day on Monday. He even threw in operation manuals for both items. I told him to expect us around 10:30, and we would return the equipment later that day or first thing the next morning."

"Great job," said Dave, "By the way, do you have your bank information handy with you in that phone notebook?"

"Sure do."

"Text it to this phone number and then break up that phone into pieces," said Dave handing Chuck the cell phone number for Roger at work.

Chuck did as Dave asked, then said, "Is this cloak and dagger stuff really necessary?"

Dave said, "I don't know, but the client expects it, so I'm playing by their rules. Let's go out to Target for more burner cell phones, and we can discuss dinner along the way."

Dave and Chuck pulled out of the Bellair entrance onto US 250 and headed east toward town. Dave decided to go through the city rather than take the By-Pass. He looked into his rear-view mirror and saw a white sedan behind him, but a large black SUV was the next car behind the white sedan. As he got to the stoplight at University Avenue and Alderman Road, he turned right to head south on Alderman Road. The white sedan kept going straight on University Avenue east, but the large black SUV turned right also and was now behind Dave, although pretty far back. Dave saw this and thought the SUV was a Cadillac Escalade based on the grill marker in front. As he went by the University dorms on his right, he decided to turn left into the Scott Stadium west parking lot. The SUV waited but then also turned left into the same parking lot. Dave went around the stadium to the parking area for the athletics ticket office and pulled into one of their parking spots as though he was there to buy some football tickets. As he got out of his car, he saw the SUV go by, and he noticed the back license plate was a government-issued plate for a GS 15, meaning the person assigned to this car was a GS 15 official or higher, which was the pretty significant status for government people. Dave moved over to the entrance door to the ticket office, and the SUV continued out of the parking lot and back onto the street leading north. Dave then returned to his car and got in without going into the ticket office.

"What was that all about," asked Chuck.

"That government SOB was following us in the black SUV, and I wanted to see if I could get a plate number. The number won't matter because the SUV is a pool vehicle used by a GS 15 employee or higher when needed. All I could see was two guys in suits and dark glasses in the front seat."

"Well, now we know that the IRS has finally caught up with you," joked Chuck trying to lighten the mood.

"I need to think about a strategy the next time I see them tailing me to make them stop and find out what the hell they want."

"Oh, you mean like having them rear-end your car?"

"Well, that's one way, but I'll come up with something. This is getting out of hand now."

Dave and Chuck completed their assigned chores at Target and Lowe's without any further disruption by the black SUV or anyone else. Then it was dinnertime. And Dave knew that Chuck was a meat and potatoes kind of guy, so he suggested they go downtown to Citizen Burger or to Boylan Heights for their burger. Which ambiance would Chuck like: a pedestrian downtown mall or near the University where more young people might be in the restaurant?

Chuck chose to be closer to young females.

Boylan Heights in early August, before the students arrived at the University, was still crowded. Dave saw several large, athletic guys there who should be on the food plan at the Virginia football facility since the team was into heavy-duty summer practices now before the season started at the end of the month. But since Chuck had his eye on a table full of good-looking females, Dave turned his attention to them also before the restaurant host asked, "How many?" Dave put up two fingers and said, "Two."

Thursday night was hoping at Boylan Heights, and the music got even louder as the evening progressed. Dave and Chuck had trouble talking to each other, which did not matter because the distractions were everywhere, and the burgers were big and juicy. Besides, the real action would not start until around 10 pm when younger folk decided to go out. And even though the young ladies smiled at both Chuck and Dave when they starred at them too long, no one was going to pay any real attention to two senior citizens cruising a college bar. So, after a couple of beers to go with their burgers, Dave and Chuck decided to put their eyeballs back into their sockets and head to Dave's house for a nightcap for old guys – Maker's Mark with one gentleman's round ice cube.

Chapter Five

On Monday, August 15, 2022, Dave and Chuck left Dave's house around 9 am and drove to the Charlottesville's Center at Belvedere on the north side of town. They used Dave's car so Richard would have a way to go home after they picked up the truck. They parked in front of the Center, locked the car with the car's fob, and went inside. Richard was standing at the main desk and talking to the receptionist. He left her and came over to Dave and Chuck.

"Good morning, brother! Who is your friend?" asked Richard.

"Hi Rich, meet Charlie Conrad, better known as Chuck." Richard and Chuck shook hands and exchanged pleasantries.

"I wish we could stay and chat, but Chuck and I have some equipment to pick up and then work on my project. We'll get together later this week for lunch, OK?" Dave said in hopes that he could get going, but not give the short straw to Richard.

"Sounds good, let's do that," said Richard.

"I will make the back-end exchange at your place later today, maybe as late as tomorrow morning after breakfast," said Dave looking to buy time for their work today.

"Semper fi," Richard said as they left toward the back door to the Center.

Dave and Chuck got into the pickup truck and turned on the ignition. Dave noticed that the gas gauge was pretty low, which was normal since the truck had not been used more than once a week since it was purchased, and with the price of gas so high in 2023, the idea was to put only what you needed in the tank for that day's use.

Dave turned right to head west on Rio Road, which took him past Albemarle County High School, where he had spent his formative youth. He pointed out the school to Chuck and said he had a good run there, even though he was a second-string player in football and basketball. But he started baseball and golf. After each turn the truck made, Dave would look into the rear-view mirror to see if any particular car was following him. So far, so good. He turned right onto Georgetown Road to go over to Barracks Road, where he turned left at that light. He then got onto the Charlottesville By-Pass heading east at that point and went all the way to the end at the east juncture of the Rivanna River and US 250. After crossing the river, he pulled into a gas station at the top of Pantops Mountain and pulled up to a pump. He looked over at the highway to notice the traffic going by and didn't see anything suspicious. He went inside the store and gave the attendant $40 cash for his pump. He got just over 8 gallons pumped before the pump clicked off at $40, and he shook his head in remembering the cost of gas when he first started to drive in 1976, roughly $1.55 per gallon then, now more than a two-fold increase.

Dave and Chuck then proceeded without further worry or checking cars in the rear-view mirror and headed to Short Pump and the Comcast field office there. During the drive, Dave summarized for Chuck the information on the origin of the Jefferson graveyard and its ownership by the Monticello Association.

"Apparently," said Dave, "Jefferson and his boyhood friend Dabney Carr rode horses through that area a lot and would read under a great oak tree there while their horses rested. They made a pact that both of them would be buried under that oak tree, and whoever died first would be put there by the survivor. Carr later married Jefferson's sister Martha but died early, when he was only 30 in 1773. To prepare the graveyard, Jefferson had a parcel 80' x 80' grubbed (cleared). Carr's burial was the first grave there, followed soon afterward by graves for three infant children of Jefferson and his wife Martha (although none of the children's graves are so marked today), then Jefferson's mother in 1776, and Martha Jefferson herself in 1782. The great oak tree survived until around 1912 and was removed a year later before it fell on the existing graves. A group of lineal descendants of Jefferson and his wife Martha bought the graveyard in 1913 from the Levy family, the then-current owner of Monticello. The Association has maintained the graveyard since that date, and additional land has been added from time to time to now encompass nearly 0.7 acre with many more burials covering about 2/3 of the available land."

When they arrived at the Comcast field office, Chuck went inside and, a few minutes later, came walking out with the GPS backpack equipment that looked like something out of Star Wars. Chuck told Dave to pull over to the garage door next to the office window. The portable GPR machine was over there and a bit heavy because the computer screen was integrated into the machine and not separate. Dave pulled over and jumped out as the garage door went up. He and Chuck lifted the GPR unit into the back of the pickup. It resembled a large walk-behind push lawnmower on four wheels but without a blade. The radar and battery housing unit replaced the engine, and it had cables stretching from there up to the juncture of the side bars where a computer screen was fastened to a plate with the controls mounted there also.

"It's heavy due to the large battery this thing requires," said Chuck. They regretted not bringing some blankets to cushion this equipment, but Chet, the head guy there, said not to worry. They could use a couple of old ones they had, which they gladly accepted. They also used some rope to stabilize the equipment from moving around too much. Chuck said he had signed for the equipment in the office and provided a credit card number in case of damage or non-return. He also had the two operating manuals, so they were free to leave, all in about 15 minutes.

As they drove back to Charlottesville, Dave summarized for Chuck the material he had downloaded Sunday on using ground penetrating radar (GPR) for detecting human bodies in graveyards. Basically, GPS has been very effective in utility work for detecting underground utilities and vaults before any digging begins on a property. The "Miss Utility" ads have been widely seen, and now all contractors are required to have a GPR report on file before any digging permit is approved for a property, all of which Chuck already knew. For a graveyard property, there was less GPR information available, and it was mostly international because, in the US, graves are left alone in perpetuity, while in England, graves can be "reused" after 100 years. That time is greatly reduced in Germany to only 25 years. Dave guessed that land was more in demand in those countries than in the US. But the big issue was whether or not there was anything left in Randolph Jefferson's grave after 200 years.

"At one end of the human remains decay scale," said Dave continuing his summary for Chuck, "are the Egyptian mummies which have remained intact for thousands of years due to the advanced embalming practices those folks had, plus coffins in a stone sarcophagus in a stone monument in an arid environment. At the other end would be there is nothing left but teeth because the body breaks down over time, starting with your brain first, then your stomach and bowels. Finally, after the soft collagen in your bones decays, the soft, hollow bones collapse into dust after 100 years or so. And, of course, there is the middle ground where we hope to be, which is some natural mummification that may have occurred, like where they are still finding bones from the colonial era in newly

51

uncovered areas at the First Baptist Church in Philadelphia and in Jamestown. So, we need a good GPR scan somehow, which will give a clue as to where we are on this spectrum with regard to Mr. Jefferson."

"You have any more good news for today, Dr. Hutchinson?" asked Chuck sarcastically.

Dave was not sure their GPR unit would give them what they needed today because the software was probably fitted for utility use and not graveyard use, which he suspected would require more specific software to include the location and position of the skeletal remains. But in his research, he knew there was a firm that did this kind of work for Civil War cemeteries and other clients, so if they didn't get some good images today, he would contact the property owner's representative and get permission to engage Topographix, LLC in Hudson, NH to do a survey of the Jefferson graveyard. The property owners ought to have one on hand anyway if they have not done this already. The GPS unit and property markings will be important to orient the Ditch Witch machine correctly to start its drilling pattern on the correct coordinates.

Dave and Chuck got back to the Charlottesville area around 1:15 pm, and Dave suggested continuing straight along I-64 west to the 5th Street exit and going through the Hardee's drive-thru there for lunch and taking it with them back one exit to the Monticello graveyard. Chuck was fine with those arrangements, and they pulled into the visitor center parking area just before 2 pm.

Dave said, "Here, put one of these hard hats on. I had two white ones made up with VSRC on them to be official." Chuck immediately opened up the inner band to make it fit his extra-large head and said, "Do I look like a stone mason now?" as he put his hat on backward.

"No, you look like a grave robber, so you stay here while I go inside and inquire about our vehicle pass.'"

"You're just worried I will try to impress a female ticket seller and then say something stupid like we're here for a body cavity check."

"Keep your pants zipped up while I'm away, lover boy," said Dave as he entered the visitor center information area.

Dave approached the ticket salesperson and said, "I'm Dave Hutchinson with VSRC, and I understand you might have a vehicle pass for me to do some initial site inspection work at the graveyard."

"Yes, Mr. Hutchinson, may I see some form of identification, please," said the female attendant. Dave showed her his driver's license, and she said, "Thank you, here is your vehicle pass for today only, and here is a map to show you where the access point is for the roadway around the main house and gardens leading to the graveyard. Any questions?" Dave shook his head, indicating none, and she said, "There is a small road leading up the west side of the graveyard where you can park, so please stay out of the main roadway, which is used by our bus trams to bring tourists to the graveyard."

"I will stay out of the way," said Dave taking the pass and leaving the visitor center.

Dave and Chuck made their way to the small side road with a circle on the west side of the graveyard and parked the pickup truck there with the equipment in the back. The first thing that both of them noticed was the fencing around the graveyard was formidable, with large 1" diameter round vertical bars forming the fencing, each one leading to a fluted top ending with a sharp spike resembling the long pikes used by the English infantry from the 12th to the 15th century against calvary charges. Fortunately, there was no need to cut a doorway into that fence as they first thought would be needed because one existed about 20 feet up from the front Southwest corner. There were a half dozen tourists milling around the outside of the graveyard, so Dave and Chuck agreed to stay in the truck until there was a lull in the number of visitors present.

About five minutes later, a tram bus stopped and picked up four of the tourists, and the other two were walking on the far east side on their way back to the visitor center on an access path there. Dave got out of the truck and went over to the lock on the west side gate. The key fit and opened the lock, and he said to Chuck, "stay here and keep people from coming in behind me," and he stepped into the graveyard proper and closed the gate behind him. He quickly paced off the square footage of open space in that Southwest corner. Dave determined there was a rectangular area about 20' x 30' available for working with a Ditch Witch inside the graveyard and pointing toward the front Southwest corner and where Randolph Jefferson's remains hopefully were buried.

Dave stepped back out of the graveyard just as the next bus tram pulled up and let out five more tourists to visit the site. He and Chuck relocked the gate and went to sit inside their pickup truck again.

Chuck said, "This is really tight on one hand, but we will not need more than one security person outside the gate. No one could break into that cemetery from anywhere else except at a gate."

"Yeah," said Dave, "we're going to have to use the most compact Ditch Witch there is, the JT5, and we will need less canvas screening than I thought and only one 10' x 10' tent inside the gate to house the Ditch Witch and our workspace stuff. Do you think a landscaping trailer could haul the JT5, and could this pickup truck pull that load? The JT5 weighs about 3800 pounds, so the total load is about 4100 pounds. I think this truck could do that, don't you?"

"I will look up the hauling capacity. Is this a 2015 Ford 250?" asked Chuck.

"I think so," said Dave, "we might have to put some wood flooring down on the landscaping trailer to keep the JT5 tracks from catching on the metal grid work on the floor. Or just rent one with the wood floor already there."

By then, another bus tram pulled up and picked up all the visitors at the graveyard. When the bus departed, Dave jumped out of the pickup and put on the GPS backpack. He got the equipment started up and picked up the positioning rod. Meanwhile, Chuck got out a hammer and several benchmark spikes, short pieces of rebar sharpened on one end, and a crosscut at the other end where the positioning rod pointed end would be placed into the crosscut for a precise GPS measurement. Chuck picked out two places on the inside of the gravel circle and drove the benchmark spikes down level with the gravel road in two locations. Dave stepped up and took the latitude and longitude measurements for GPS data for each of these new benchmarks. They moved over to the west gate, unlocked it, and stepped in and repeated that process for three more new benchmark spikes, one next to the Southwest corner, one next to an existing gravestone just inside the gate, and the last one by one of the stone bases for a main fence post midway between the west gate and the Southwest corner. Dave finished all of these GPS data points and returned the GPS backpack and positioning rod to the pickup truck as Chuck relocked the west gate.

They were back inside the truck when the next bus tram pulled up, and two people got out to visit the graveyard. "I can see why the drilling will only be done at night," said Chuck, "too much activity during the day here."

"We will need to figure out some kind of shuttle service where only one van is parked here at any one time," Dave said. "I doubt if the Foundation is going to allow us more than one vehicle pass a day, and I need to think about whether to get more keys to this gate or put a combination lock on this gate. I'm leaning toward the combination lock to avoid a bunch of keys being outstanding and not being able to account for them.:

"Good choice," Chuck said, "I like that approach also. Do you want to do the GPR sweep now that there are no visitors again?"

"I'm wondering if it really will help us anyway since it's probably fitted for metal objects and pipe rather than cemetery use," Dave said.

"We won't know unless we try. Isn't that what you always taught field guys?" Chuck said, smiling.

"Yeah, you're right. Don't prejudge the data or the results."

The next bus tram stopped, but no one got off, so as it pulled away, Dave and Chuck got the GPR unit out of the truck and pushed it over to the west gate. After going inside the graveyard, Dave turned the unit on and checked the signal, which looked like sine waves, until it saw a disturbance, then it created a slight wave within the sine wave. But Dave walked up and down the 20' x 30' area in ten passes without showing any disturbance at all in the sine wave pattern.

"Nothing," he said to Chuck on the last pass, and they went over to the truck and put the GPR machine back into the bed of the truck just as another bus tram pulled up and unloaded six visitors for the graveyard.

They drove the equipment back to the Comcast field office in Short Pump, making it there just before 5 pm and closing. They stayed in that area for dinner rather than fight the traffic headed west of Richmond. After dinner, they returned to Dave's house. The next day, Chuck left with instructions to begin to look into the staffing for the project based on seeing the tight location. Dave exchanged the pickup truck at Richard's apartment for his own SUV and went back to his house.

Dave called Richard on his personal cell phone to let him know that the truck was back in its usual spot and to see if he wanted to have lunch any time later that week. But he got Richard's voicemail and then left those messages.

Then Dave used his burner phone to text Roger Pettit that he needed another lunch meeting to include Jon Coolidge. Roger texted back the next day, saying he and Jon would meet him at Farmington on Tuesday, the 23rd of August, at noon. At that luncheon, Dave summarized the status of the project to date. "First of all," he said, "Chuck and I were able to do our preliminary work without anyone seeing that we were inside the graveyard. That took some luck and timing to accomplish since the bus tram service is regular but unpredictable in its arrivals and whether or not any tourist wants to get off and visit the graveyard. I want to return to this aspect of the project in a moment. Second, we were able to place five benchmarks for future use, two outside the fence line and three inside. Third, our early GPR results were insufficient to determine if there are any bodily remains in that Southwest corner of the graveyard. Jon, has your Association ever had a cemetery survey done before with specialized GPR software for just cemeteries?"

"I'm fairly certain that we have not done that simply because we still have plenty of room remaining for burials there, and the need has not arisen before," replied Jon, "do you think that would make a difference?"

"Based on what I know and have read, it's an absolute must," said Dave, "we need to know if there is an unmarked grave in that corner, and, if so, are there any remains there sufficient to warrant either exhumation or a non-exhumation way to access them. There is a firm in Hudson, NH, which specializes in this kind of cemetery GPR and has a long list of Civil War cemeteries and private cemeteries as past customers. I think it would take them a half-day for the survey of 600 square feet and probably a week to analyze the results. I don't have any idea of the cost, but whatever it is, I think it would be worth it now for this project as well as later on for your association. And I don't have any idea of when they could do the work."

"Go ahead and line this up as soon as possible and run the cost by Roger. I trust both of you to know whether the cost is reasonable. I would prefer that you were there when they do the work, not only to let them in but to answer any prying questions about what is going on."

"I will follow up with that firm," said Dave, "and if they are going to do the work, I will personally be there to oversee it. Returning now to my first concern, which is the constant flow of tourists visiting the graveyard and the current ruse we have used with the Foundation of work being considered to repoint some of the gravestone markings. I am very uncomfortable with using this ruse going forward because none of the work we are starting to set up with others or plan for ourselves will be toward repointing gravestones, so sooner or later, that ruse will be exposed in some fashion to the Foundation. I understand your desire to keep the project secret from the public, but keeping it secret from the Foundation is another matter entirely, and I don't see how we can do that over the course of a couple of months of drilling and getting our people to and from this work site."

"What do you propose as an alternative," asked Roger.

"I think we should have a meeting with the Foundation president, maybe one of his top aides, and their counsel, to explain that we will be investigating the vacant area in the Southwest corner of the graveyard to see if there are human remains there and, if there are, then we intend to try to extract dental DNA from those remains to identify who it might be. I don't think we have to say at this point we believe that Randolph Jefferson's remains might be there. And we will use cemetery-specific GPR for the first step, sort of like a high-level maintenance project to see what available gravesites still remain in that original section of the graveyard."

"I had hoped we could keep the Foundation out of this project," said Jon, "but I see your point about the difficulty of doing that over a prolonged period and trying to have our people and contractors come and go during that period is bound to raise their interest and perhaps their ire if we don't pony up the truth at the beginning. I could live with a meeting with them for that purpose. Roger, would they sign a non-disclosure agreement if we promised to give them a first chance to see the results if there are any, before we disclose them to the public?"

"A legal document might raise their level of concern about what we hope to find," answered Roger, "but maybe Harrison Battle and I could craft something of a gentlemen's agreement that the matters discussed would be held in confidence by only the people in that meeting."

"I could live with that arrangement," said Jon, "so it would be three people from our side and three people from their side, and we should be able to track where any leak occurred if it came to that."

Roger said, "I will call Harrison after we know that this specialized GPR firm can do the work and when, so we can set up a meeting prior to their arrival. I think it would be wise to film the specialty firm if they end up doing the work, Dave, so can you handle that job with a hand-held camera from our office?"

"Sure, I can take care of that feature since I will be letting them into the graveyard if they come for this small job," replied Dave.

"Thanks for all you are doing on this project, Dave," said Jon as he stood up to leave.

That afternoon, Dave called the Topographix, LLC office and spoke to the president of the company. Dave gave him the rough dimensions of the cemetery area to be surveyed, which consisted of about 600 square feet, with emphasis on pinpointing one particular grave and the position of the skeletal remains there. The president said they normally don't do small jobs like the one being described, but his firm has a contract with the Chancellorsville Civil War Cemetery in early October that he could tie the Jefferson Cemetery job into that job. The cost would be roughly $20,000 for that kind of area, plus expenses for a team of two to come to Charlottesville in the company's van with equipment. Since the company personnel would already be in the general area, he estimated those expenses at $2000 for a one-day turnaround. The base fee would include interpretations and analyses for a specific gravesite. They could do the job at the end of the first week of October if this matter was signed up fairly quickly and a deposit of one-half, or $10,000, was sent to them. The deposit would be partially refunded if the contract was canceled before September 20th, but no refund of the deposit money would be made thereafter if the contract was canceled.

Dave said to fax all that information to the property owner's legal counsel, who had power of attorney to sign on behalf of the property owner. And he gave out Roger Pettit's name and fax number. After hanging up, he texted Roger to alert him to the incoming fax from the company with the contract details and that he thought the arrangements were reasonable and fair under the circumstances. Roger then texted back, "Great news."

A week later, Roger texted Dave on his regular cell phone that a meeting had been arranged with three people from the Foundation plus Jon for Wednesday, September 7th, at 2 pm in his Charlottesville office.

Chapter Six

September 7, 2022

Dave had lunch on September 7th at Timberlake's Drugstore café and then walked up a block to the office of Pettit and Brown on Market Street, arriving there at about 1:45 pm for the scheduled 2 pm meeting with the Foundation folks. He was shown into Roger's office since Roger was on his way back from lunch himself. Jon Coolidge, the current president of the Monticello Association, was already there.

Hello, Dave," said Jon, "How are things with you?"

"Fine," said Dave, "Do you have any notion of who we are meeting with today?"

"I would suspect that the president of the Foundation, Clayton Lawrence, will be here and perhaps his senior historian, Roberta Carter-Jones, who took over that role from Denise Parker after she retired about three years ago right before the Covid shutdown. I have met Clay before, but not Carter-Jones. Parker and the other strong-willed ladies from the Foundation staff published a lot of books and papers about the slavery life at Monticello and championed the 25-year effort named Getting Word, which documented the oral histories of Jefferson's enslaved families. These ladies and outside authors were able to push these oral histories to a status of historical fact even though all of them have inaccuracies and misinformation that cannot be corroborated. Together with the tainted DNA study by Dr. Foster, were enough to hang poor Mr. Jefferson with the label of the father of the six children of Sally Hemings."

Roger entered the office at that point and said that the others were now in their conference room. He suggested that he would introduce everyone and then let Jon take over to state what the Association wanted to do in the Southwest corner of the graveyard.

As they entered the conference room, as happens in most meetings with "sides," all three of the Foundation participants were on one side of the conference table and Jon and Dave on the other side with Roger at the end, sort of like a referee or master of ceremonies. Roger said, "Thank you for being able to meet with us. Let me introduce everyone; I am Roger Pettit, counsel for the Monticello Association. To my left is Harrison Battle, counsel for the Thomas Jefferson Foundation, then Clayton Lawrence, current president of the Foundation, and I believe the lady is Roberta Carter-Jones, the Foundation's senior historian. To my right is Jonathan Coolidge, the current president of the Monticello Association, and then Dave Hutchinson, a certified project manager and former Vice President of Project Management for Comcast. I have spoken with Harrison about the confidential nature of this meeting, and we have agreed to dispense with a formal non-disclosure agreement in favor of an understanding that what we talk about today is confidential and may not be discussed with anyone outside of the six people here today. Have I correctly stated the understanding, Harrison?"

"Yes, you have, Roger." Said Battle.

Jon began, "Thank all of you for coming. I asked Roger to set this meeting up to give you advanced notice of a project the Association wants to undertake in the front Southwest corner of the graveyard. We believe that there is at least one, and perhaps two, graves there that are unmarked. We have a tentative contract with a New Hampshire firm using their proprietary ground penetrating radar equipment specific for cemetery investigations to survey about 600 square feet of that corner to see if any human remains are there. If their findings disclose human remains there, we will then proceed to try to get dental DNA from those remains, either by exhumation or non-exhumation means, in order to attempt to identify those remains. The first part of this investigation is currently scheduled for the end of the first week in October, and we will notify you of the results when we get them. If there is a reason to continue with the second part, we will meet again with you and provide a full plan for that part of the investigation."

"May I ask if this proposed first part with GPR equipment will require any closure of the graveyard to visitors?" asked Clayton Lawrence.

"A very good question, Clay," replied Jon, "I will let Dave explain how a GPR survey is done."

"The quick answer to your question is there will not be any closure or limits placed on visitors to the graveyard that isn't already there, meaning access to the inside of the graveyard itself," said Dave. "The GPR machine looks like a large tricycle with two wheels in the back, and one in the front with the radar unit slung close to the ground between the front and back wheels. The firm will stake out 2-foot-wide strips of the ground to be surveyed using a normal white cloth tape. This simply keeps the machine going over new ground and not wavering along the way. These 600 square feet of area will take about ½ day to survey, and visitors will see the work going on inside but not be prevented from seeing any existing plaques or informational markers and especially the Jefferson grave obelisk. I will be on-site to let the contractors into the graveyard through the west gate and to lock up after they leave."

"What is it that you hope to achieve by this project?" asked Battle.

"We have wondered for some time," replied Jon, "Why that Southwest corner appears to be vacant, so we want to make sure it really is vacant. When Dave was retained, he knew of this New

Hampshire company who could help us without having to drill core sample holes and perhaps damage something if there is something there we haven't known about previously."

"Let me add," said Dave, "That all we need at this point is a vehicle pass for me and one for the firm. Their equipment comes in a van-like vehicle no larger than my pickup truck. And we will park on the short lane and circle on the west side near the west gate to stay out of the way of your bus trams that day."

"I think we can see this through one more pass, Harrison," said Lawrence, "it might turn up something very exciting. As long as we get to see the results before any other work is approved or proceeds, I think the Foundation will not be affected by this first part."

"I have a question if I can ask it?" said Carter-Jones. Hearing no objections, she asked, "Who do you think is buried there?"

"We don't have any firm idea if anyone is buried there, but we think it's prudent to establish *IF* there are any human remains there in case there is a future request by a lineal descendant of Thomas Jefferson Randolph who wants to be buried in that part of the original cemetery."

"Roger," said Battle, "call me a few days before you need the two-vehicle passes set up, and we will look forward to another meeting when you have the results of this GPR survey to review with us."

"Thank you, Harrison, I will do that, and we should get the survey results about a week after the work is actually done, so I will be in touch with you when those results are on hand."

Everyone shook hands, although the handshake from Carter-Jones had that limp, fingers only, feel to it like she knew something was not right. After the Foundation folks left and Jon and Dave were in Roger's office, Jon said, "Carter-Jones must know about the Jefferson letter to his sister indicating that Randolph Jefferson's remains may have been buried in that Southwest corner."

"Well, even if she does," said Roger, "they can't do anything about it right now because we are working on our property and not interfering in their rights in any way.

Dave left Roger's office feeling like the Foundation was going to be a problem for the project going forward, but maybe he would be proven wrong, or maybe there wouldn't be any remains identified in the Southwest corner of the graveyard. And Dave didn't like the maybe game.

Chapter Seven

Mid-September, 2022

It was a rainy fall day in Charlottesville, with intermittent showers forecasted throughout the day and little likelihood of sun or even significant dry periods during the day. Dave decided to stay indoors and download as much material as possible on dental DNA. He sat down with a nice Chardonnay wine from Barboursville Vineyard and read and re-read those materials, and grouped them into organized "buckets."

He picked up the first bucket and began to summarize the information in writing on blank sheets of paper. This summary approach was a lifelong habit of his to put the information into his brain and have a summary page at the same time. He thought that finding information on dental DNA would be difficult, but, in fact, with the library of the world at your fingertips on a computer, that information was readily available. In particular, Dave liked the source *Journal of Forensic Dental Science*. Their semi-annual edition in December 2010 was especially helpful because it was right on point: *"Dental DNA fingerprinting in identification of human remains."*

Dave started with the classic dictionary definition of DNA, which is Deoxyribonucleic acid (abbreviated DNA), which is the molecule that carries the genetic information for the development and functioning of an organism. DNA is made of two linked strands that wind around each other to resemble a twisted ladder — a shape known as a double helix. Early use of DNA for identification was limited to sources found in blood and body organ tissue, but by around 1995, harder substances like bone marrow and teeth became fertile ground for DNA material. Teeth are encased in a sealed box of lasting durability, and even one tooth can provide valuable information about the person to whom the tooth belongs. The most common use of dental DNA today is DNA fingerprinting, where identification of human remains is not possible through visual means or past dental records. For plane crashes, collapsed buildings, charred bodies, and skeletons from long-ago deceased persons, dental DNA has opened the door to identifications not thought possible until recently.

Dave continued to summarize: Teeth vary in form and size, but all have a similar microscopic tissue structure. Dentin is the name given to material below a tooth's enamel and is the connective tissue between the pulp of the tooth and enamel. It is the structural steel of the tooth, so to speak. The pulp below the dentin contains the nerves and blood vessels of the tooth which eventually combine into two root canals in the form of prongs below each tooth. It is the nucleated blood components in the pulp chamber that are the rich sources of DNA for dental fingerprinting and identification. In long-ago deceased bodies, after the gum line and other bodily oral tissues have decayed, the tooth pulp remains in place due to its protective encasement by the dentin and enamel of the teeth.

Dental DNA has been used on an Egyptian mummy to identify a female ruler (lacking the male Y-chromosome), victims of the 2004 Indian Ocean tsunami, and an incinerated body. A tooth from a male blood relative of Thomas Jefferson might solve the long and controversial issue of the paternity of Eston Hemings, the last son of Sally Hemings, scientifically. The DNA profile of Eston Hemings was part of the 1998 Foster DNA study. Dave concluded his notes by writing a question for the eventual forensic dentist about whether sawing off a tooth versus full normal extraction by pliers would in any way damage the pulp for a dental DNA sample.

September was one of Dave's favorite months in Charlottesville. Maybe it was because it was the start of another football season for high schools and colleges, or maybe it was the early fall breaks in the humidity or even the foliage of deciduous trees about to turn reds and yellows in the foothills of the Blue Ridge Mountains. But Dave didn't like maybe games, so he believed it was his favorite time due to the great golf weather and the courses, like Farmington, were in prime shape for club championships. Dave was still a nine handicap, although he wasn't playing at that level now because he was busy with his project. But the next step in that project was waiting on the cemetery GPR survey team, which would be in town in early October to survey the Southwest corner of the Jefferson graveyard. So, for every great golf day in September, Dave was on the course or the practice tee to sharpen his game. The first two rounds of the Farmington club championships were to be held the weekend of September 24-25, followed by the last two rounds on October 1-2, when there was no home Virginia football game. Qualifying for the championship flight would be done on September 18th, but Dave had decided to skip that this year and just be in the First Flight where his handicap put him. Each flight had 16 openings, but the First Flight also would have four of the twenty golfers who signed up for the Championship Flight qualifying but failed to qualify and were assigned to the First Flight. Dave was one of 12 others to sign up for the First Flight based on single-digit golf handicaps.

On Saturday, September 24th, Dave played Horace Webb, a five-handicap player who failed to qualify for the Championship Flight. Webb was a big guy who hit the ball a long way but was not as nimble as Dave around the greens, so Dave practiced his short game a lot on Friday before that match, and it paid off, as Dave won the match on the 17th hole, 2 up with 1 hole to play. The next day, he played Brian Duvall, a distant cousin of pro David Duvall. Brian had won his first match 7 and 6 by shooting even par on his own ball without considering any handicap differential. Dave was worried that Brian might be on top of his game, and that turned out to be correct because Dave was 2 down after the first two holes when

Brian birdied both holes 1 and 2. Dave always disliked holes 3 and 4 at Farmington because they were sort of squeezed into the existing topography rather than looking like nature intended the holes to be there. But Brian's drive on 3 found the trees on the right, where golf balls go to die. So, Dave hit a long iron for his drive and played that hole defensively, and won it with a bogey. The match then went back in forth as each player got hot and then made a mistake to lose the advantage. After 15 holes, Brian had a 1-up advantage over Dave. But the 16th hole at Farmington is a devious, double-snake-curved, par-5 hole, and Brian pulled his drive into the valley of sin on the left, another place where golf balls go to die, and Dave played the hole in par to even the match going to the short, downhill, par-3 17th hole. When they got to the tee box at the top of the hill, a member of the Farmington golf staff was there and motioned Brian to come over. After a few opening sentences, Brian yelled out, "Is she alright?" Apparently, Brian's wife had been in an auto accident and had some non-life-threatening injuries but was being taken to the University Hospital for treatment of bruises and observation.

Brian said, "I am forfeiting the match to go to the hospital. I'm sorry to have to leave in such a rush."

Dave said, "Absolutely not, the match will be suspended until we can finish it during the coming week, and I will not accept a forfeit. You need to be with your wife now, and golf can wait until you know more about her recovery."

"That's very decent of you, Dave," said Brian as he stepped into the club's cart. "I will let the golf shop know if and when we can finish later this week. Thank you for your sportsmanship."

They sped off to get back to the golf shop. Dave decided not to play the last two holes and drove back to the pro shop and watched Brian leave in his car.

The following Wednesday, Dave and Brian met at 5 pm at Farmington to finish their match. Brian said his wife did not stay overnight and was sore the next day but fine considering the condition of the car. An impaired driver had come through a stop sign and hit her car broadside on the passenger side, fortunately, and not on the driver's side. Dave teed off first and hit his iron shot into the bunker on the right side of the green, but Brian put his tee shot in a perfect spot below the pin on the left. Dave had enough green to work with, but sand trap play was not his specialty, and he hit it out short and below the pin. He missed his par putt and conceded Brian's 7' birdie putt uphill. The match moved to the 18th hole, which Dave had to win to extend the match. But Brian was back on his game and closed out Dave with a par to win the match 1 up. As they shook hands, Brian said what a generous thing Dave had done to not accept a forfeit, and he appreciated Dave's sportsmanship. Dave wished Brian good luck in the remaining matches.

Dave stayed at Farmington for dinner, and several golf pals and the head professional came up to him to say what a great gesture he had made for the good of golf to not accept a forfeit but allow Brian to finish the match at a later date. He got several free drinks out of that gesture, but it didn't make his evening feel better. As he pulled out of the Farmington property and turned left onto US 250 east toward town, the black SUV was sitting on the shoulder of the road further west and started up to fall in behind a red pickup truck which was now behind Dave. His first thought was, "why not? Nothing else is going right tonight." The more Dave stewed about his bad luck, the angrier it made him. When he turned right into the Bellair subdivision, he hit his brakes hard and jumped out of the car, looking for a large stone to throw. The red pickup truck went by, and the black SUV started to turn right but saw that Dave had stopped, and it immediately swerved back into the through lane and sped up to avoid hitting another car. Dave didn't have any rocks to throw, so he just yelled, "Keep the hell away from me." He thought of the line from the Tom Hanks movie *Forest Gump* when Gump said, "Sometimes, there just aren't enough rocks."

The next morning, Chuck called, which helped Dave refocus on the project. Dave answered Chuck's call,

"This is Ben Dover. If you want me to do that now, press 1; if you really want to talk to Eileen, press 2. All others, hang up and seek professional help."

"This is Rusty Nail. I want to speak to the gatekeeper," said Chuck.

"She is not here; she ran off with the key master," replied Dave.

"Glad you're in a good mood. I wanted to hear the results of the Foundation meeting," said Chuck, "you have been AWOL for a while."

"Yeah, I tried to play golf with the big boys and got my butt handed to me, and the black SUV tried to rear-end my car but missed."

"Sounds like everything is normal in little ole Charlottesville," Chuck said.

"The Foundation meeting went pretty well, and they are cautious about what our end game is but willing to roll the dice so far. Their senior historian suspects we know more than we actually know. The cemetery GPR specialist will be here next week to do the survey work on the vacant 600 square feet in the Southwest corner of the graveyard. Their report will either keep the project going or kill it if we don't find any bones there."

"I will let you go find a Bloody Mary somewhere now," said Chuck, "it sounds like the project has entered a quiet time for two or three weeks, so I might take off and go fishing again if that's ok with you?"

"Sure, it's no sense making plans now when we don't know the end game yet and whether the Foundation will impede our work even if we find some interesting bones in the graveyard.

"Ha," Chuck said, "Every graveyard has interesting bones. Hopefully, there will be some in our graveyard. If I catch any tuna, I will bring some tuna bones with me next trip and scatter them around to confuse the Foundation. They will think we uncovered a pre-historic site. Take care, old friend."

"Who you calling old, friend," said Dave, but Chuck had hung up.

Chapter Eight

Dave met the team from Topographix, LLC, at the Monticello visitor center on October 5th at 10 am. He had retrieved two vehicle passes from the ticket office and then had them follow him to the west side of the graveyard. Their GPR equipment was quite different from the one Dave and Chuck had used from the Comcast field office. This one looked a bit like an oversized tricycle, sort of like the line-marking machines used for baseball fields. It had two wheels in the back and one in front, and the radar unit was positioned close to the ground in a metal chassis slung between the front and back wheels. There was a large battery pack on another rack slightly above the radar unit, and it had a computer at the top of the frame at the back wheels. The guys who arrived with the equipment said this job was a "piece of cake," and they had done over 300 cemeteries combined between them. They said the key difference was their proprietary software, developed by their president, who was an IT professional and a Civil War buff.

Dave showed them the 600-square-foot area to be surveyed and pointed out the specific grave site area where Randolph Jefferson's remains might be. He also showed them the survey benchmark nails he and Chuck had set up. They said that would help make their results even better because all that data could be fed into their computer. Their resulting maps and any skeletal remains images would be almost in three dimensions with specific latitude, longitude, and depth data for critical points like the skeletal head and other body parts. Dave told them the property owner wanted him to film them at various times doing this work, and he hoped they wouldn't mind. They said to leave the rest to them, so Dave went back to his car and got his hand-held camera that Roger had lent him and then took some film of them for the next 3 hours. They first laid out a grid pattern with white tape in 2-feet widths starting from the west side fence, numbering the lanes 1-10, with 1 being the closest to the west side fence. Each of the tapes had letters on the tape every 2 feet starting with "A" so that the exact Southwest corner at the intersection of both fence lines would be A1 consisting of 4 square feet, B1 would be the next 4 square feet along the west side fence and so on. They then placed their GPR machine in the A1 square and began to scan all the space in lane 1 next to the west side fence and repeated this next lane over (lane 2) and so forth until they had done all 600 square feet needing to be surveyed. The work was slow and tedious, but they seemed to be going back and forth in lanes 4, 5, and 6, especially between the early letters C through G.

They stopped at 12:30 pm and came back to their van to retrieve some lunches and beverages they had packed for the day. They agreed they had about 1 more hour once they finished their lunch break because they wanted to do a second scan of just the specific grave site where some remains might be. Dave asked if that was an indication that their first results were faulty in some way. They said it was standard practice to have two sets of data when a particular grave site was being investigated. They thought the first set was fine, and it showed the presence of some bone fragments still there, but not to worry, all that would be in their report. Dave silently wished he had thought of bringing some snacks or lunch with him today. He had brought the latest "Joe Pickett" novel by CJ Box but felt he could not concentrate on it and film the survey team at the same time for their second pass.

The survey team finished up shortly before 2 pm and then left. Dave re-locked the gate and went to the nearest place to get some fast food quickly. During the day, there were five or six inquiries from visitors as to what the Topographix guys were doing, and Dave answered they were scanning that vacant area to be sure there were no actual graves or buried remains there. Silently, he was hoping that this survey would be as conclusive as he expected. Otherwise, the property owner might have to use the backup plan of outright exhumation or forget the whole thing if there were no teeth or bone fragments remaining in that area of the graveyard. There was still a lot to do for a drilling solution, but Dave was tired and went home to read his CJ Box book and have a nice glass of Pinot Noir. He felt the book and wine were just right for dosing off on the couch.

Two days later, Dave called Chuck on a new burner phone to update him on the status of the project. Chuck didn't pick up, perhaps because it was a new phone number to him, so Dave left a message for Chuck to call back when it was convenient.

When Chuck called back, it was nearly 5 pm on Friday, and Dave was on the driving range at Farmington, hitting some balls. Since he didn't carry the burner phone with him to Farmington, he missed the call. And after staying for dinner there with some golf friends, he got home too late to call Chuck back. So, he waited until Saturday morning and called Chuck again. Someone partially answered the phone and then apparently dropped it, and Dave heard female giggles, and then a female voice said, "This is the Fairy Godmother, your wish is my pleasure…, wait a minute, that's not right," then Chuck got on the phone and said, "Hi there, partner, sorry about that interruption, how are you?"

"Well, not as good as you, it sounds like," replied Dave.

"Oh, that's just Susan," Chuck said, and Dave heard a hand slap and the female voice say, "What do you mean, *just Susan*," with the emphasis on the last two words.

Dave knew this was not a good time, so he said, "Call me Monday. I will be around here all day."

"10-4, boss," said Chuck, and he hung up.

Around 10 am on Monday, Dave's burner phone rang, and he knew it must be Chuck, so he answered,

"This is the Charlottesville Public Works Commission, press one if you have a complaint about your plumbing; press two if you have gas; press seven if you want a stoplight repaired on your street. And for all other callers, press zero."

Chuck repeated his oft-used line of not having a digital phone to press and then said, "Good morning. Sorry about Saturday morning. Susan is a friend who sleeps over from time to time."

"No problem," said Dave. And he gave him a summary of the new GPR survey of the cemetery and then said, "We should know the results in another couple of weeks, and I will let you know as soon as I hear. The results will be sent to Roger first by fax, so he will pass them along when they arrive."

While Dave was on the phone with Chuck, there was a knock on his front door. It had an ominous sound to it, hard like a man would do, and just two serious even raps. He told Chuck he needed to call him back later, and he put the burner phone down under a magazine. He walked to the front door and opened it.

There was the same large, black SUV with the motor running on the street in front of Dave's house and a man now standing on his front porch dressed in a dark suit, white shirt, rep tie, and aviator sunglasses still covering his eyes.

"Mr. Hutchinson, my name is Special Agent Davidson, and I'm with the NSA. May I come in and talk to you?"

"What's this in reference to Agent Davidson, and why have you been following me for the last three months?" Dave said to put confrontational pressure on the visitor.

"That's why I'm here, Mr. Hutchinson. May I come in rather than stand here in the heat?" Davidson repeated.

"Come on in and sit down. Would you like some iced tea or a soda?"

"No, thanks."

"How about some water?"

"No, thanks anyway. I'm here because your bank reported to the IRS that you had received a $15,000 wire transfer from an international source three months ago, and you also have received, over the last two months, additional wire transfers in excess of $25,000 over that two-month period. The IRS turned this information over to us because we have a field office on the north side of town, and we were asked to investigate these transfers."

"Before you go any further," Dave said, "Let me put my phone on video and record this visit."

"There is no need for you to do that, Mr. Hutchinson."

After turning on his personal cell phone to video, Dave said, "Yes, I think there is, and your man out there in the SUV is probably recording this conversation also, and you didn't inform me that you are wearing a wiretap for that purpose. I believe that is against the law, isn't it? Don't you have to read me my Miranda rights?" And Dave sat down as far away as possible from Davidson.

"Miranda rights are used only if an arrest is underway and I'm not here to arrest you," said Davidson, and after a dramatic pause, continued, "*Yet.* And yes, I am recording our conversation today."

"Thought so." said Dave, "Just for the record, I haven't done anything illegal to warrant your following me or being here."

"Well, now that we have those preliminaries out of the way, what is the purpose of those wire transfers you have received from an international source?"

"I thought the legislation to require banks to report transactions greater than $600 to the IRS did not pass, so why are you here?" Dave continued to press the legitimacy of this intrusion.

"Perhaps you are not aware that after the Russia-Ukraine War started last February, the President signed an Executive Order to seize all US-based assets of the Russian Premier Putin and his oligarchy associates. Part of that order included a requirement for all US branches of any bank, foreign or domestic, to report any wire transfer into or out of US accounts equal to or greater than (a) $10,000 in one transaction or (b) $25,000 in the aggregate for all transactions over a two-month time period in order to prevent the seized assets from being moved in and out of bogus accounts. So, I am here because your name is on both lists. Now, once again, what is the nature of the money you have received by wire transfer from an international source, Mr. Hutchinson?" And Davidson slightly emphasized Dave's name for effect.

"I will not answer any of your questions, Agent Davidson, because I do not think this Executive Order is valid as it relates to American citizens. My lawyer will be in touch with your head man at NSA north of town." Dave was equally emphatic in his ending.

"I must warn you that your lack of cooperation with a valid investigation could result in fines and/or imprisonment."

"Is that threat also in the Executive Order?"

"No, that is standard NSA department protocol for uncooperative people who hinder a valid investigation."

Dave stood up, meaning this conversation was over, and said, "I will ask you to leave now, Agent Davidson, and stop harassing me by following me all over Charlottesville. Now that we have equal warnings. Good day to you."

After getting to Dave's front door and opening it, Davidson put his aviator sunglasses back on and said, "I am sorry you will not cooperate with me now, but you will stay on the watch list, and I may be back to see you after we develop more information on your wire transfers."

Dave shut the front door, almost pushing Davidson off the front porch. He shut off his cell phone and saved the video he had just made. He got out the burner cell phone he had hidden under the magazine and texted Roger Pettit: "Hi, this is Dave. I just had a visit from NSA. Let's have lunch at the usual place when it's convenient for you. Let me know just the date and time on this cell phone."

When he looked up after sending that text, the black SUV was gone. Dave wondered how people in those positions slept at night. How in the world did our country get into this sad shape? He called Chuck back and updated him on the visitor from the ghost of Christmases past. Chuck said he didn't have any more to report on his drilling and security plans, and he hoped that Dave could stay straight. Chuck said, "I have a 12-step program you can follow to avoid federal agents, Dave," to which Dave just said, "Ha," and hung up.

Roger called back the next day and said Jon would not be back in town until October 27th, and that would be the next luncheon at Farmington unless Dave had urgent matters. Dave said no, his update could wait until then. Roger asked Dave to tell him more about the visit from Special Agent Davidson. Dave filled him in on the entire encounter, and Roger concluded that Davidson still didn't have much and the project was better off just ignoring him unless

Davidson interfered again by another visit or stopping Dave while tailing him, that would be harassment, and Roger would get involved then.

On October 27th, Dave met with Roger and Jon at Farmington. After finishing lunch, Roger surprised both of them by having the survey results from Topographix, LLC, which had arrived that morning. He passed a copy to Jon and a copy to Dave and said,

"The only thing I could tell from all this is that they have identified human remains in that corner and at least one location in the middle of that area had a skull and a few bone remnants. There is evidence of another unmarked grave disturbance next to that one but without identifiable bones. And there is evidence of three or four smaller grave disturbances nearer to Jefferson's grouping, and they also don't have any remaining identifiable bones. The report says we should expect the bones still there to be quite brittle. The one skull is about 3.5 feet below the surface, slightly tilted to one side, with the right jaw slightly higher than the left. It is positioned away from the south main fence line with the other bones between the skull and that fence line to suggest that the feet may have been closer to the fence line than the head. There are a lot of data points on their maps which I hope Dave can figure out, so here you go."

Dave looked over the maps first and said, "At first glance, these will help us a lot, and it sounds like extraction will be just a matter of pulling on a tooth, and it will break off, so we need to be careful and not ruin the tooth pulp. I will get several copies of the coordinates map enlarged at a copy center where I can use the equipment myself and have one or two of the enlarged versions on the job site. As we drill the access hole, we can plot our drilling GPS data points on one of these copies to project our progress and stay in alignment. By adding the depth of the current drill progress to the azimuth longitude and latitude, we can have a visual almost in hopes of arriving slightly next to the right jaw for a dental DNA sample. I am amazed at what this survey company can do, and, Jon, this was well worth the cost, in my opinion."

Jon said, "I guess this means we move on to parts two and three of the project regarding a forensic dentist."

Dave said, "I agree in principle, but there are two issues I would like to discuss first. I know that your organization frowns on the exhumation, but with the brittle bones there, exhuming this skull as an archaeological dig would be the easiest and least costly way to get the DNA of whoever was there. At this point, we don't know for sure who is there, and we might be involving a lot of extra expense for no real benefit in knowledge if it turns out it's not Randolph Jefferson. And finally, there is so little remaining of the person there; exhuming the skull is not like grave robbing or disturbing the dead because there is so little left after 200 years. The second issue has to do with a meeting with the Foundation, which we should have once we have settled on our approach to accessing the skull there."

Jon paused for what seemed like a long time, then sighed and said, "I really can't make this decision myself without checking with others in the Association and especially the anonymous sponsor funding this work. I hear what you are saying, Dave, but this would be an unprecedented move for us. We have never had an archeological dig within the graveyard in our 110-year history of ownership. I certainly don't want to turn over control of this effort to the Foundation, which has archeological experience. In addition, Dave, you would be out of your project management element, I think. This is a very difficult decision, and I need some time to think more about it and contact other Association members. What do you think, Roger?"

Roger said, "It's a difficult decision for sure, Jon, and we could send this information to the Foundation and simply say we are formulating our plans and will meet with them when we have a plan worth discussing. Harrison already called once last week, asking if we had received the survey report. Another possibility might be to have the archeology pros from Jamestown look at this report and our site and give us opinions about the two methods of accessing the skull."

Jon replied, "I like that approach to get a professional opinion from the Jamestown folks, so we don't have to depend on the Foundation's opinions. Dave, do you have any problems with this approach first?"

"None at all," said Dave, "I think it makes very good sense to work slowly at this point. Perhaps you can poll your members as to exhumation if the archeology pros say that is the best way, and maybe Roger and I can find some contacts at Jamestown to bring into the fold on our side for a professional opinion."

"Fine, then," said Jon, "let's move on this quickly. Roger, you send the Foundation a copy of the report saying we will schedule a meeting when we have our plans completed, and I will poll some of the membership."

"I will make some phone calls this afternoon to see who might be a contact for reaching out to the Jamestown folks," said Roger as they left the Farmington Grill.

The next morning, Dave was having breakfast at his house when his phone signaled a text message from Roger.

"Call me," it said.

When Dave called Roger, he was on another phone call, but his secretary asked Dave to leave a number where Dave could be reached. Dave gave her one of the burner cell phone numbers to use. About ten minutes later, that cell phone rang, and Dave answered,

"Good morning, Roger. How are you?"

"Good morning to you, Dave," Roger said, "I have been able to talk to Dr. Ronald Bishop, Director of Archeology for the Jamestown Rediscovery Foundation Staff, and he is willing to come to Charlottesville on Monday, October 31st, to meet you at the Monticello visitor center to see the site and then meet me afterward. He happens to be coming to Richmond this weekend and can meet you at 10 am at the visitor center on Monday. You all can then meet me for lunch at Farmington after the site visit has been completed, say around noon. I have called Harrison Battle to arrange for a vehicle pass in your name for Monday."

"Great work, Roger," said Dave, "I will be at the visitor center a little before 10 am on Monday."

On Monday, October 31st, Dave was at the Monticello visitor center at 9:45 am and picked up his vehicle pass from the ticket office. He then was standing outside looking at the prospective single guys who could possibly be Dr. Ronald Bishop when a lady walked up to him and said,

"Good morning, Mr. Hutchinson, you probably don't remember e, but I am Roberta Carter-Jones. We met last month in Roger Pettit's office?" she said with a question mark.

"Yes, good morning to you. I am waiting to meet someone here to look at the graveyard site," said Dave.

"Yes, I know, you are waiting for Dr. Bishop. We are old friends. The archeology world is a small one, and he has been here to help us on some of our recent digs around Monticello. Harrison Battle faxed us the copy of the GPR survey report you had done on the Southwest corner of the graveyard, and it shows a very promising new archeological find, so It's no wonder you want some expert advice about whether or not to start a new dig there."

Just as Carter-Jones finished her sentence, a distinguished professorial man in a straw hat walked up and said,

"Good morning, Roberta. How are you?" And turning to Dave, he said, "and you must be Dave Hutchinson."

"Hello, Dr. Ron," said Taylor-Jones, "I am fine. Dave and I were just talking about the small community of people involved in archeological digs."

"Hello, Dr. Bishop," said Dave, "Yes, my name is Dave Hutchinson." Dave thought to himself that 'Dr. Ron' by Carter-Jones seemed a little too familiar.

"I guess I should have told your Mr. Pettit that I have done consulting work for the Thomas Jefferson Foundation, but I didn't think about it then. I don't think it presents any conflict of interest since there are two separate organizations. But we can discuss that with Roger at lunch. Nice to see you again, Roberta."

Dave and Dr. Bishop rode in Dave's car around to the west fence parking area at the graveyard, and Dave unlocked the west gate. He walked to the general area of the location of the unmarked grave where a skull and some bones remained as determined by the cemetery survey, a copy of which he gave to Dr. Bishop for his use that morning.

"To start with," said Dr. Bishop, "this is a small area, and you would not want more than three active diggers, and all the digging needs to be manual without any mechanical backhoe. All the material needs to be stripped in 6" layers and screened to make sure any artifacts are collected and recorded along the way. I assume you are interested in reaching the skull to collect dental DNA material for identification?"

Dave wasn't sure whether to answer such a direct question but decided to hedge by saying, "that is certainly part of the owner's plan."

"The archeology staff at the TJ Foundation has plenty of experience in processing this type of area. Are you considering using them for this dig?"

Dave again hesitated before answering, "We haven't thought that far ahead yet. We just want an idea of what is involved if we decide to start a dig here." Dave began to suspect that the casual meeting with Carter-Jones at the visitor center was planned.

"A dig of this importance needs a highly trained and professional staff along with a slow process. My guess is this work should take at least a month and maybe as much as three months to uncover everything that is here. I also assume you will want to shield the work from the public by canvas and maybe a tent, but there is room to that and not impact the tourist value of seeing the Jefferson gravesite itself."

Dave didn't answer, so Dr. Bishop continued by pulling out a small straight tube and sticking it into the ground. He then twisted it and pulled it back out. "It looks like normal Virginia mountainside soil, some topsoil with a predominance of clay below that. Hand digging will be slow and difficult in spurts; that is the reason for the lengthy time element. What have you determined about the disturbances over there closer to Jefferson's actual gravesite?"

"We haven't determined anything yet about that area," said Dave, "it's possible that was the location of Jefferson's infant children's graves."

"Every gravesite has an archeological story to tell, Dave, and the Association should consider a large enough dig to answer why those disturbances occurred over there and the one next to the skull here. There may be remnants of coffins in each area even though the human remains are no longer with us. There might be other artifacts in those coffins to help fill in the details of the daily lives of the people back then."

"Is there anything else about this site that comes to your mind, Dr. Bishop?" asked Dave.

"Well, I would guess that horizontal drilling might be more difficult due to the roots from the tree over there," he said, pointing to the large oak tree about 15 feet away.

Dave thought to himself, *this guy has been set up from the beginning. The Foundation already wants to control the dig if that happens or suggests that horizontal drilling shouldn't be done as an alternative. They know my background and have planted a guy here to steer us to them by his professional opinion.* But Dave decided to keep all this to himself and see how the lunch played out.

"That's about all I need to report to Roger at lunch," Dr. Bishop said, "shall I follow you back to Farmington? I kind of know the way, but following you will be best for both of us."

"That will be fine with me," said Dave.

At lunch, Dr. Bishop outlined all the aspects of a potential dig at the Jefferson graveyard for Roger. He carefully avoided talking about the meeting with Taylor-Jones at the visitor center and his admonition about horizontal drilling. Dr. Bishop concluded by saying, "in my professional opinion, your organization should consider a complete dig of the entire 600 square feet of the Southwest corner utilizing the experienced archeological staff at the TJ Foundation already on site."

"Thank you for your time, Dr. Bishop. Please send me an invoice for your time and expenses, so we can reimburse you," said Roger, standing and shaking his hand goodbye.

After Dr. Bishop left, Dave said, "Roger, I think this was a setup from the beginning."

"How so?" said Roger.

"First of all, he is and has been a consultant for the Foundation. Next, Roberta Carter-Jones was there to greet him as we met at the visitor center this morning and knew him well enough to call him 'Dr. Ron.' Third, he is recommending the Foundation as the dig coordinator so they can control the data and information, and they want the entire area to be done, not just the area where the skull is located. And finally, he recommended that we should avoid horizontal drilling due to tree roots, so they know my background at Comcast."

"Well, you must have bitten off half your tongue during lunch with that spiel by him. Two can play that same game, and by that, I mean I have talked to Jon this morning and his polling of some of the other members of the Association and especially the paying sponsor, and they do not want an archeological dig of any kind in the graveyard. So, your horizontal drilling has to produce the dental DNA from that skull so we can wrap up this mystery."

"I am pleasantly surprised by this turn of events," Dave replied. "Now, we need that forensic dentist idea you had earlier.

"Yes, I was hoping that news might energize you." said Roger, "I have a friend who is the dean of the Dental School at the Medical College of Virginia in Richmond. He might either be the right guy or know someone else he could recommend. Let me give him a call and set up an appointment for you to discuss the project with him. I know him well enough that we don't have to worry about a legal document unless he is going to be the actual dentist on the project. I will call you tomorrow with a date that works for him. His name is Dr. Solomon Bernstein, and we've been on a couple of advisory boards together in the past."

"Sounds like a good start," said Dave, "now we need to set up a meeting with the three people from the Foundation and report that we have decided to investigate the skull area for dental DNA."

"I will set up a meeting with them after talking to Jon again today. I will get back to you when that meeting is held in my office, and you should have a full drilling plan ready to put forward to them."

"That will be a pleasure, Roger," said Dave, and they left Farmington.

Chapter Nine

November 2022

Since Roger had lined up a meeting with Dr. Solomon Bernstein, the dean of the Medical College of Virginia dental school, for the following Tuesday, on a lark, Dave decided to text Richard Dunleavy for Lucy Carlisle's phone number. It couldn't hurt to see if she wanted to have lunch that day when he was in Richmond, could it? When Rich texted her number back, he phoned Lucy on his regular cell phone.

"Hello," Lucy said as though she wasn't sure whether or not to answer the phone.

"Lucy, this is a voice from the past. It's Dave Hutchinson calling."

"Well, Lord have mercy, Dave. How are you? What's it been, like, 40 years?"

"I'm fine, Lucy. How are you and, more importantly, how is your mother doing? I heard from Richard Dunleavy that she had a stroke a couple of months ago."

"I'm fine. It's such a pleasant shock to hear from you. My mother is doing a little better now, thank you, she still has some partial paralysis on her left side which makes walking a little more difficult. But she has full use of her right hand for writing and taking care of herself. She lives in the independent living group at the Colonnades Continuing Care Facility in town, but it's getting closer to having her move up to assisted living status."

"Well, at least she is still part of the living group. Glad to hear that, and Rich said your husband recently passed away. I was so sorry to hear that. Was he sick a long time?"

"He got Covid in 2020. He was an attorney here in town and continued to go to the office to work through the pandemic, even when he began to feel feverous and nauseous. I begged him to stay home, but he was stubborn, like all men, and he died after being in the hospital for only a week in October 2020. I got a milder case of it right after that and was almost ready to go into the hospital myself around Thanksgiving, but by the grace of God and some therapeutics, I got over it, and now I have a natural immunity to some extent."

"Lucy, the reason I am calling is to see if you want to have lunch, and I mean just lunch, next Tuesday? I have a meeting in downtown Richmond that morning, and we could meet in town or somewhere else that's convenient for you."

"Why Dave, that's very charming of you to say just lunch, and I would like to do that and catch up on everything. I live closer to Short Pump. Maybe something out that way would work on your way back to Charlottesville?"

"How about Mangiamo's, the Italian place in Short Pump, at, say, 12:30 pm then."

"That will be fine with me, and it's been good to hear from you, Dave. I look forward to next Tuesday in Short Pump."

"Great, Lucy, I will look forward to it also. Take care, bye," and Dave hung up, almost sweating since he had not asked a woman out in over five years.

The following Tuesday, Dave left his house at 9 am for Richmond. As he pulled onto US 250 from the Bellair subdivision, he saw a black SUV in the parking lot of the Exxon station across the street. That car quickly pulled out of the parking lot, crossed over to the eastbound lanes of US 250 and turned left, and began to follow Dave onto the By-Pass heading east through town. Dave decided what the hell. He was not going to evade this car anymore, so he just went directly east on the By-Pass. The black SUV passed him on the By-Pass, and he saw that it was a Chevy Tahoe rather than a Cadillac Escalade, and it had a normal Virginia license plate. He felt foolish about his initial thoughts and that he had been reduced to seeing a ghost in every closet because of this project. He arrived at the Virginia Medical College dental school parking lot around 10:45 am, about 15 minutes before his appointment with Dean Bernstein.

It took about 15 minutes to find the dean's office, so he was right on time. The secretary said he was expected and it would be just a couple of minutes, and the dean was on the phone right then.

When he was ushered into the dean's office, Dave said,

"Dr. Bernstein, I'm Dave Hutchinson and thank you for seeing me. I know that Roger Pettit contacted you on my behalf, and I am grateful for his introduction."

"Nice to meet you, Dave," said Dr. Bernstein, "Roger and I are old friends and have been on a couple of boards together through appointments by the Governor in the past. How can I help you?" and he motioned for Dave to sit down.

Sitting down, Dave said, "I am working on a project to extract two teeth from a person who died and was buried many years ago. And this has to be done remotely through a tube inserted into the grave area where the person's remains rest. That's all I can tell you about the project at this time. I wanted to know if the tools and skills exist today to be able to do that from a dental extraction standpoint?"

"Well, that is certainly one of the most unusual requests I have had in a long time, but the short answer is a qualified yes, meaning under the right circumstances and with the right person. Why is it necessary to do this from a remote location? Why not just exhume the remains, to begin with, and extract the tooth directly?"

"I can't disclose the reason behind the remote access part of this problem, but what are the right circumstances you feel would be needed?"

"For starters, how long is the cable connection from the controls to the remains, because I don't know of any situation where this has been done farther than 10 feet away, like, say, micro-surgery in a radiation environment using instruments controlled remotely from a sealed environment. And second, how many other instruments need to be in the cable access, and how much room do they take up?"

"Good questions," Dave replied, "we will need a light source in the cable to visually see what we are doing and a camera to view and record everything, and we might have to change the active end of the main tool from cutting to collecting or to have a mild vacuum to remove fallen dirt or other debris. We might be talking as much as 15 feet away for the remote controls and video screen."

"Yikes, sounds like a lot of clutter in the cable and extremely difficult circumstances."

"Yes, but it's important to know if this can be done with the right person under the control levers and if there is no time pressure like what might be present in an actual surgical procedure. We are not time constrained, in other words. And it's also important to be able to do this without errors or shortcuts because it will be documented for future review."

"So, it's a first-time event, it sounds like," said Dr. Bernstein with some excitement in his voice, "and it sounds like a DNA search to me."

"Very much so," said Dave, "and it may need to be done at night in the cold outdoors."

"Goodness, you are really making history here. And it couldn't be more difficult if you had tried."

Dave decided to go broke, "Would you be interested in being that person?"

"I might be once I heard all the details. Are you able to provide those now?"

"No, sir, I can't, but I know a way we can line this up for you to hear all the details within a week and then let you decide if you want to participate or not."

"Let me know when you are ready to provide those details. Thanksgiving break is coming up in two weeks, and after that, we have exams here, so I will be busy until Christmas unless you can do this, say next Monday or Tuesday here at my office."

"Thank you for those open dates, Dr. Bernstein. I should be able to set something up for then or call and say we have moved on to another solution. Thank you again for your time today."

"My pleasure and have a good day, Dave," said Bernstein.

As Dave left the dean's office, he didn't know whether to feel triumphant or depressed. That's the way all aspects of this project have gone so far. It was a little before noon, so he proceeded to Mangiamo's in Short Pump.

When Dave walked into Mangiamo's at precisely 12:30 pm, he wondered how he would know Lucy Carlisle, whom he hadn't seen in over 40 years. What did she look like, grey hair or dyed, heavy or trimmed, and so forth? Just then, a woman came up to him at the host desk and said,

"I would recognize you anywhere, Dave Hutchinson. I'm Lucy," she said with almost a child-like glee. "You haven't changed very much at all."

"Hello, Lucy. Thank you for making this easier to find you," said Dave. "You look terrific, like Rich said."

"Oh? And what else did he say?" said Lucy with a sly grin.

"Just that and the information about your husband's passing and your mother's stroke."

"Ok, I will let you off the hook. I have a table over here," and she pointed over to a booth in a quiet corner of the restaurant. "And since you said this was 'just lunch,' let's make it a Dutch treat."

"Well, I didn't mean it that way. I insist on picking up the tab."

"OK, I won't fight it. It's just nice to see you," she said smilingly. "I know you went to the engineering school in Virginia and married Marsha. What else has happened along the way?"

Before Dave could launch into a short summary, the waitress arrived, and they ordered drinks and looked over the menu for a few minutes. Dave then told Lucy about Comcast and Marsha's problems, the divorce, his work focus, and his recent retirement and relocation back to Charlottesville. By that time, the waitress had returned with their drinks, and they ordered lunch.

"So, how about you," asked Dave after the waitress left.

"After Albemarle, I went to VCU here in Richmond and was a journalism major. I graduated on time and got a job with the *Richmond Times Dispatch* as a cub reporter, so to speak. At first, it was social stuff, who was marrying who or engaged to whom. Then I got to move into the news division and started covering follow-up investigative reporting on accidents and murders. I took three years off for time to get married and have two kids. I have a daughter who is married and lives here in Richmond with her husband and one grandchild. And I have a son who lives in Wyoming. He graduated from Virginia Tech with a degree in forestry management and is now a Park Ranger in Yellowstone Park. I was lucky enough to have my mother available for child care, so I was able to go back to the news desk at the *Times Dispatch.* By then, the internet had started its invasion into the news part of the newspaper business, so I switched over to covering the Governor and the state house people here. After my husband, Bob made partner in his law firm, I decided I had enough of a career, so I retired in 2015."

"Wow, impressive," said Dave, "I don't have any children," and he paused, "that I know of," he said smiling, "I guess work interfered too much with a family life, something I regret to this day, but can't do anything about that now at this stage of my life."

The food arrived, so they settled down to eat and think of other topics for a later conversation. After finishing up lunch, and with Lucy putting half of her sandwich into a box to go, the dishes were cleared when she said,

"Dave, this has been fun, but after you called last week, I got a call from my daughter asking me if I could babysit for her at 3 pm today, and, of course, I said yes because children only stay little for a short time and I like being a grandmother and a part of this next generation. I really hope you will call again, and we will have to do 'lunch' again, even if it's in Charlottesville."

"It has been fun, and I will definitely call you again. It might be just before Christmas, but even if that doesn't work out, I will call you so we can stay in touch."

Lucy gave Dave an appreciative kiss on the cheek and said, "Stay in touch," and then left the restaurant.

Dave drove back to Charlottesville, rethinking all that Lucy had said, trying to rationalize clues as to how she viewed this renewed relationship or if it was a relationship at all. Anyway, he thought, the lunch turned out better than he had hoped, and indeed Lucy looked terrific. He tried to block out a number of memories of when they were dating in high school, but Lucy was far more confident and in charge of her life than he remembered her from those days long ago.

After Dave got back to his house, he used a burner phone to text Roger Pettit that he had news to share about the project. About an hour later, he got a text back from Roger that Jon was heading to town on Thursday night, November 17[th,] and he hoped Dave was available for a meeting with the Foundation on Friday at 10:30 am in his office and lunch afterward at Farmington. Dave texted back that yes, he would see them on Friday at 10:30 am in Roger's office. He then broke that phone into pieces and discarded the pieces like all previous times.

On Wednesday, November 16[th,] Dave thought about hitting some golf balls on the Farmington driving range because he had missed the last two months of the Tuesday "Nine and Dine" golf events there and also missed the last three Saturday rounds with his regular foursome. But just then, he got a text from Chuck Conrad asking Dave to call him on his burner cell phone and provide the number.

When he called the number, Chuck answered by saying, "This is God's older brother. If you have called to make an appointment, we are full for the next 20 years."

"Well, that's good news," said Dave, "I won't have to worry about doing the right things here to get into Heaven. How are you, *old* friend?" with an emphasis on old.

"Pretty good. The doctors say my liver has a stage 3 disease condition, but the good news is that there are 30 stages to liver disease." Switching subjects quickly, he said, "How are you doing keeping away from the FBI or IRS or whoever is tailing you?"

"Good," said Dave, "What's on your mind?"

"I have gotten a crack drilling crew lined up of four newly retired field guys. They only know that a possible job exists for about two months after the first of next year. They are people I know personally and understand it might be under Spartan conditions out of town."

"That is good news, Chuck. I am having another lunch meeting with our clients and Roger on Friday, and I know they will be happy to hear that news. Anything else?"

"One other thing," said Chuck, "I have been thinking about this security personnel issue and believe we should use our hand-picked guys rather than some rent-a-cops who may or may not be suitable and willing to keep their mouths shut off shift."

"Good thinking there. What do you propose in its place?" asked Dave.

"I'm thinking about some out-of-town private detective types who have licenses to carry a weapon and are used to zipping their lips up when off the job. I know a couple of guys here in New Jersey with universal licenses to carry concealed weapons, and we can round up four more, provide them with housing and an official-looking security uniform, and be able to trust them. I am thinking we need two shifts of two guys each where in each shift, they are working one-on and one-off, rotating every hour. Whatcha think?"

"I like it," replied Dave, "keep working on that angle until Christmas, and let's make up our mind after that."

"10-4, Coach, put me in."

"Right, and go to the next one of your two remaining phones after today, and you know what to do with the present one. I have the numbers for those other two."

"Got it. Have a nice Thanksgiving, I'm going out deep sea fishing again next week, so I won't be available from the 22nd to the 27th."

"Try not to drown, OK? Have fun and take care. Bye." Dave spent the next couple of hours detailing in his mind how the horizontal drilling program would be done, the security program, and how to shuttle his people, so there was only one van at the site except for his specific visits in his truck.

On Friday, November 18th, Dave met with Roger and Jon in Roger's office for a few minutes to go over the game plan for the morning meeting with the Foundation folks. Dave said all he needed from the Foundation was access to the site for a van every day for roughly six weeks plus a continuous pass for his truck over that same time or perhaps eight total weeks with one week before and one week after the workforce on site. Jon said he would handle the issue

99

of declining the archeological dig and use of the Foundation's experienced excavators.

Harrison Battle was a little late for the 10:30 am start time, so everyone waited until he arrived at 10:45 am and then assembled in Roger's conference room. Roger welcomed everyone and said, "I am sorry the report from the cemetery survey took more time than anyone expected, and due to travel schedules, we could not meet until today."

Jon then said, "The Association has looked long and hard at this issue of exhumation by an archeological dig and any other method of identifying the human remains disclosed by the cemetery survey. Further, we are very aware of the outstanding field archeologists that the Foundation possesses and has used with great results in the past on archeological digs at Monticello. But our only interest lies in identifying the skull we now believe is there in that vacant Southwest corner, and our membership is opposed to any archeological dig inside the graveyard. Therefore, we have decided to proceed with a horizontal drilling program to reach the skull carefully to expose the right jawline for a dental DNA sample to be taken and then analyzed to determine the identity of the person there."

"I can understand your organization's reluctance for an exhumation, Jon," said Clayton Lawrence, "but think of the opportunity that this situation presents to determine not only the identity of the skull there but also where Jefferson's infant children may have been buried and what might have been next to the skull in that area. These opportunities don't come along except once in a generation."

"That may be, Clay," said Jon, "but our membership is not interested in a total search of the vacant area nor in any form of exhumation of the skull site that involves an open archeological dig.

100

We are comfortable only with a minimally invasive intrusion by horizontal drilling to expose just the area around the skull for a DNA sample, as difficult as that will be. Dave, why don't you lay out the basics of the drilling plan."

Dave said, "Horizontal drilling will be done by the most compact Ditch Witch machine on the market with precision fluid drilling until we get close, and then we will switch to dry drilling. The Ditch Witch will be totally on Association property and be sheltered by a 10' x 10' tent. We will insert support piping that will give us access to the front drill head with a camera and light to slowly access the right jaw based on the GPS positioning disclosed in the cemetery survey. We will have a forensic dentist do the actual tooth extraction with the proper legal DNA seals and chain of custody for transport to the FBI lab in Quantico. We will have a security guard posted at the west side gate 24 hours a day during the actual work time, and we will install canvas shielding on the first 20 feet along the south fence line and the first 30 feet along the west side of the graveyard fencing. We will complete that rectangle with additional canvas held up by poles and stakes for supports on the other two legs inside the graveyard. And we will drill only at night after the Monticello grounds have been closed, with no active work done during daylight hours. We will need one continuous pass for a passenger van to be on site along that west side and one continuous pass for my truck which will come and go at various times and park in that same west area and circle. And we expect the actual work to begin in February 2023 and end about six weeks later."

Jon then finished by saying, "we are prepared to meet with you at any time some interruption of your property rights occurs during this two-month work period and to meet with you prior to any public announcement of any findings we discover should they be of importance to you."

"Well, that is considerate of you," said Clayton, "But all this activity at night puts a burden on our own security force. And I must say how disappointed I am in your unwillingness to join forces with us to investigate this very exciting opportunity for more information on the entire Jefferson story at Monticello."

Dave added, "Our night crew will come in at 7 pm and leave at 7 am each day unless the weather prevents us from drilling. In that case, we would notify you during the day that no one other than the night security force of two men will be there that night. None of our people need to leave the immediate area, even for a restroom, we will have chemical toilets on site for our people, and the security forces will be trained in what to say to any tourists who happen to question why the canvas shielding during a daytime visit."

"Roger," said Harrison Battle, "I don't think any of us can give your organization a response to this news today. We need to meet with our other officers and staff and then get back to you. If we come up with any more questions, I will pass them on to you for your consideration. With Thanksgiving approaching, I don't see us responding until the second week in December at the earliest."

"That's fair," said Roger, "We will await your response then."

Then Carter-Jones blurted out, "You think that the remains there are those of Randolph Jefferson, don't you?" Dave was surprised by the inquisition tone in her voice.

"Whether we think that or don't think that is immaterial, Ms. Carter-Jones," said Jon, "we want to conduct an investigation on our property and not interfere with any of your property rights except to have one or two vehicles be able to access the work site for two months. We will not hide nor hinder any visitor from seeing the gravesite of Thomas Jefferson. Our request should not be a burden on the Foundation for all the years of joint cooperation with you for visitors to see the gravesite of Thomas Jefferson."

Carter-Jones then crossed her arms in a defiant gesture, but Lawrence touched her shoulder as he stood up, signaling the end of the meeting. There was nothing further either side could say. Roger did wish everyone a happy Thanksgiving. After the Foundation folks left, Dave said, "I will drive separately and meet you at Farmington for lunch."

At lunch, Jon said, "The Foundation really doesn't want us to do this investigation and are trying to find a way to control it if it has to happen."

Dave and Roger agreed. Roger then said, "IT will be interesting to see what roadblocks they try to use since the only thing we are asking for is continuous vehicle passes for two vehicles, and even those vehicles will be out of the way."

Dave briefed them about the meeting with Dr. Bernstein and his possible interest in being the forensic dentist the project would need later. Jon asked Roger if Dr. Bernstein was current enough to be up on the latest techniques, and Roger said,

"Even as Dean, Sol has continued to supervise directly the Friday clinic lab where the students see various indigent patients for their work experience in school. That clinical experience runs the whole gambit of dental problems because poor people generally don't take care of their teeth, and they seek out the clinic for free service when their teeth finally hurt them. They don't mind the student mistakes or first-time efforts because Sol is right there guiding them to prevent a huge problem from developing."

"Ok," said Jon, "Do you want to set up another visit with him and go through the preliminaries to discuss the difficulty of this project?"

"Sure," said Roger, "I will call his office again and see when he is available. Do you have any restrictions, Dave?"

"No, I can make it most any time up to Thanksgiving," Dave replied.

Dave then briefed them on Chuck's progress, and they both liked the idea of using out-of-town private detective types for the security teams. He also reported that he had another tailing by the black SUV and that it had a GS 15 government plate on the car. Furthermore, an NSA Agent by the name of Davidson had visited him at his house and wanted to know the origin of the wire transfers sent to Dave, but there had been no further incidents of tailing or interruption since that visit.

On Tuesday of Thanksgiving week, Dave got a text message from Roger that a meeting with Dr. Bernstein actually had been set up for the Tuesday after Thanksgiving at 11 am and that Dave should meet him at his office at 9:30 to go in one car. Dave then called Chuck on his burner phone and left him a message that the clients liked the work to date on the project and that Chuck should proceed to round up detectives for the security team. Dave also suggested that Chuck looks into houses for rent as far east from town as Zion's Crossroads because there may not be many of them, and he thought the work crew ought to be in one and the security teams in the other even if it meant the "hot bunk" approach for that latter group. Dave preferred that both groups not be too near town to avoid them being tempted to go out on the town for some reason, dining or other.

On the Saturday after Thanksgiving, Dave played golf but was disappointed in his play even though he hadn't played in a month. His regular foursome was happy to see his poor play because it meant he lost all three matches against the rest of the foursome. They usually teamed up in pairs, but Dave didn't want to be a burden on his regular partner after his hiatus from playing, so he suggested a $5 Nassau bet against each one of the other three, meaning $5 on the front nine, $5 on the back nine and $5 on the total score against each of the other three players. He lost all three ways to each other player, meaning he lost $45, and they even made him pay for the drinks at the club grill afterward. Some friends thought Dave, but he deserved the beat-down because he had been too focused on work.

When he left the Farmington property and turned left onto US 250 to head back toward town, he noticed a black car on the shoulder of the road close to the entrance to Boar's Head Inn further west on US 250. That car got back on the road and was following Dave again, even though he only had to go a short distance to the Bellair subdivision. Dave was already in a foul mood but decided to have some fun, so he went past the Bellair entrance and continued toward town. At the Alderman Road light, he turned left to cross the railroad bridge there and then turned left again at the next light to head out Sandridge Road toward the By-Pass. The black SUV continued to follow him. Once on the By-Pass heading east, he got onto US 29 heading north, then got off that at the Hydraulic Road light and headed west on Hydraulic Road. All the while, the black SUV was following him. He turned into the Stonefield shopping area and then went to park at Trader Joe's to get some take-home meals while he was out having all this fun. When he got back into his car, he didn't see the black SUV, and it did not reappear on the way home. So much for cloak and dagger that day.

At home, Dave made two calls on his personal cell phone. The first was to Richard Dunleavy to see if he was back in from spending

Thanksgiving with his brother's family in Maryland, but Rich didn't answer, and Dave didn't leave a message. Then Dave called Lucy.

"Hello, stranger," Lucy said when answering, "how are you?"

"Just fine, Lucy," said Dave, "how are you doing, and how is your mother doing?"

"I'm fine, and Mom is doing about the same as before, Dave. She had Thanksgiving with her Colonnade neighbors, and I went over to my daughter's house for Thanksgiving dinner in the middle of the day. You do that when you have little ones around who can't stay up very well for an evening meal. How was your Thanksgiving?"

"I went back to New Jersey for a couple of days and played some golf there and then here after I got back," stretching the truth some. "The reason I'm calling," he continued, "Is to see if you want to have lunch this coming Tuesday. I have to be in Richmond again that morning, and we could meet again at Mangiamo's."

"Well, that sounds delightful, Dave. Let's make another 'just lunch' then" Lucy punched the last three words in a playful manner, "what time is good for you?"

"Let's make it 1 pm this time. The morning meeting might require more time this go round."

"Ok, 1 pm it is," Lucy said, "I will be looking forward to it."

"Me too. See you then, Lucy, bye now," Lucy Carlisle, he thought, I wonder where this is heading, but she seems eager to build a new relationship.

Dave then called Roger but had to leave a message, which contained three parts: (1) that he would meet him at Dr. Bernstein's office because he was having lunch later with a friend in Richmond, (2) he assumed Roger would bring a filled-in confidentiality and non-disclosure agreement to the meeting, and (3) he also wanted Roger to bring him a letter addressed to Central Virginia Tent Company, explaining that Roger represented both the property owner, Monticello Association and the contractor, VSRC in the person of David Hutchinson, for restorative work to do on the property. Dave explained he would use this introduction in early December to establish the VSRC confidentiality and non-disclosure agreement with the tent company, have them install the tents and screening canvas on a date to be supplied by Dave, and then take it all down when the project is complete. That would save Dave's crew from doing that work and maybe damaging something and from buying step ladders and mall hammers for installation.

On Tuesday after Thanksgiving, Dave headed out of his sub-division and couldn't believe it. There was the black SUV in the Exxon parking lot again across the street. It crossed over two lanes of traffic to turn left and fell in behind Dave with two other cars in between. Dave wanted to stop his car and find out why they were still following him but decided to ignore them and headed east on the By-Pass up to Pantops and then to eastbound I-64 toward Richmond. Different cars were behind him, but the black SUV stayed with him until he turned left to get onto I-64 east.

Dave arrived at Dr. Bernstein's office at 10:50 am and sat down to wait for Roger, who arrived at 11:05. Dr. Bernstein was finishing up a meeting in his conference room and finally sat down with both of them at 11:20 am.

"Sol, I understand you want to hear the details of Dave's project," said Roger, "and I sent you by courier a blank copy of a confidentiality and non-disclosure agreement that needs to be signed before Dave can tell you those details. I brought a filled-in copy for you to sign and can tell you that I am involved to the extent that I represent the property owner in this matter and Dave, as to his participation in it, if that will help you understand the parties involved."

"Roger, that helps tremendously, and I will sign the document, but that doesn't mean I am the right person at the end of the day," Bernstein said.

Roger said, "Sol, the dental part of this work will be done under an initial retainer of $7,000 for the first 20 hours of service, and that will be wired to your bank account, so give me that data before we leave today if you are still interested later. Once you go past 20 hours, another $7,000 will be deposited, and so on. If the project is successful, there will likely be a press conference to attend and public announcements and interviews later. I hope this money arrangement is sufficient for your time?"

"That will be fine, Roger," said Bernstein, "and if I take this on, I will send you a statement each time to account for the hours."

Dave then filled in Bernstein on the details about the cemetery, the location and orientation of the mysterious skull, the report from Topographix, and their belief that the bones remaining would be quite brittle and closed when the actual drilling is likely to start in mid-February.

"Frankly, Dr. Bernstein," said Dave, "I am concerned that if, and it's a big if, we are able to get the main cable to the correct place above the jaw bone, the final dentistry work has to be done at a right angle to the cable. Can that be done?"

"Every dentist is trained to do work at odd angles in the mouth, only using a mirror to see where a drill is touching, so I don't think the angle will present any problems. Will the cable have a side opening of any kind?"

"Yes, I expect so," said Dave, "once we get slightly past the area we want, we will withdraw the drilling unit and pull the support piping slightly back. We will then insert a slightly smaller diameter thin-walled pipe all the way from the start to the end of the drilled-out section. That second pipe will have two half-inch tubes for inserting a camera into one and a LED light into the other, plus a 3" dental instrument tube for the final extraction and holding onto the tooth when needed. The front head of this entire unit will have a ten-inch-long slot for access to the skull remains. If that section needs to be rotated to give direct access to the right jaw, we will back up the section or extend it more if we are long or short of the right jaw target. We hope to have teeth numbers 2 and 3 fully exposed at that point to simplify extracting the teeth. Extracting the teeth is another problem in my mind, and maybe you can help. If the teeth are as brittle at the jaw line as the Topographix report suggests and they are broken off as an extraction procedure, will that provide enough tooth pulp for a proper DNA sample?"

"I believe so," said Bernstein, "but it will need to be done extremely carefully. I will confirm that with another forensic dentist on the faculty here. I assume you will want a qualified lab to do the analysis, and the FBI lab located in Quantico is the best in the business for DNA work. And I know the correct procedures to take for establishing a legal chain of custody in sending the sample to the lab. By the way, Roger, we will need an independent witness to observe the sample taking and evidence envelope sealing. Do you have another lawyer friend from another firm in Charlottesville who can be that independent witness?"

"I will come up with one when that time comes. By the way, Sol," added Roger, "This entire project will be filmed, and we might want to film you and the witness taking the sample to the FBI lab and turning it over to them with the proper chain of custody signatures and seals."

"That's fine," said Bernstein, "Now, if you will excuse me, I have an important donor meeting and lunch to attend. I will be back to you, Roger, with any news. Based on what I know now, I think I would like to be a part of this historic event."

Dave and Roger both said their goodbyes and, on the way out to their cars, concluded that this project might be a go after all. Roger said he would call Jon and fill him in on today's results.

Dave let Roger leave the parking lot first, and then he proceeded to Short Pump to have lunch with Lucy.

Dave arrived at Mangiamo's in Short Pump right at 1 pm and saw Lucy standing at the host desk.

"There you are," Lucy said, "I was hoping to get the same table we had before, and it depended on you being on time, or they might have to seat other people there. We're in luck again," she said excitedly as she touched both of Dave's hands and then held onto one of them to walk him to the table.

After ordering their drinks, Dave asked, "How is your mother doing now?"

"She seems OK." replied Lucy, "I talked to her this morning, and she still has a physical therapist session three times a week, and I think there has been some progress. She says she walks with a cane now without assistance from the therapist, but I want to see that myself when I visit her next time. By the way, I should have asked earlier, how about your parents? Are they still living?"

Dave answered, "No, Dad died in his sleep in 1991. The doctors said there were no signs of a heart attack or other direct causation of death, so they decided it was due to sleep apnea since his brain was starved of oxygen. There seems to be a growing number of people with sleep apnea dating to that time and continuing through to today. Mom said he snored a great deal, so much so that she often slept in a different room, and snoring is a material correlation with sleep apnea. In fact, Mom said she slept in a different room the night he died. She felt awful about that, but the doctor said she would not have noticed anything because people with apnea just stop breathing long enough for the body to shut down from lack of oxygen. There would not have been any physical body jerking or a reflex action by the limbs during this oxygen deprivation."

"Oh, that must have been awful for your mother, Dave, and for you, too, to not be there when your dad died. I'm so sorry," Lucy offered. "Bob snored a lot also, and I think I do too sometimes." Lunch arrived then, which helped break the mood slightly. While eating their sandwiches, they shared some light chit-chat about the weather getting colder and Lucy's granddaughter. After finishing most of their sandwiches, Dave said,

"Mom died from pancreatic cancer in 1995. She had overlooked some discolorations in her bowel movements for a couple of months. After some tests, the doctors said the cancer had metastasized everywhere, and they didn't see any value in even trying the Whipple procedure on her. She died three months later. I took a leave of absence to be with her when she entered hospice care. Those were the dark days for me, along with Marsha's issues, but all that's past history now. One of the things that I took away from Dad's death was that sleep studies have shown there is some value to having one of those beds with an adjustable base to elevate your head and feet if you want. I snored a lot then also, according to Marsha, so I had two sleep studies done in New Jersey, which were inconclusive because my oxygen levels never dropped very much. But when I moved to Charlottesville, I decided to get one of those king-sized beds with an adjustable base," he said with a coy smile with an emphasis on 'king-sized,' "They even have individual dual controls so each person can control the firmness of the mattress and desired elevation to eliminate most snoring" he said continuing the coy tone in hopes of lightening the mood with Lucy.

"Why Dave Hutchinson," Lucy said with the same coy smile, understanding the hidden meaning, "Are you inviting me to your house for a sleepover?"

Continuing the coy slant, Dave replied, "Well, we could consider it a scientific experiment in snoring reduction."

"Ha," said Lucy, "And we should follow the science today, right?"

"Definitely," said Dave, but then deciding he had pushed the envelope far enough for now, continued, "As nice as this has been, I need to get back to handle a few things on the project before dark. It's been another great time, Lucy."

They got up to leave, and she kissed him on the cheek and said, "Stay in touch. We might have a scientific experiment to do later," hoping he was not playing with her emotions.

"I will," Dave said, and she left the restaurant.

Dave tried to avoid psychoanalyzing Lucy's responses on the drive back to Charlottesville. At least she had not said no, so there was a future hope. As Andy Dufrane said in the movie *Shawshank Redemption*, hope is always a good thing.

Chapter Ten

December 2022

On Thursday, December 1st Dave went to the Charlottesville Materials Company location in town to talk to someone familiar with custom fabrication for a project his company was doing. Dave sat down with the main CAD designer for the materials company and described his trenching company's project in general terms. Dave pulled out a drawing of the end diameters of what he needed for each type of pipe and a plan view of all of it together, plus a drawing of the proposed "head" piece for the main instrument pipe. He would need several different piping sections where the thinner the wall structure, the better, but don't sacrifice strength. The CAD designer said that usually meant thin-walled PVC.

First, Dave needed 20 feet of 5-inch outside diameter piping in 5 four-foot sections, each with a male and female end for screwing one section into the next. Second, he would need 20 feet of 4-inch outside diameter piping the same way, meaning in 4-foot sections, each with a male and female end, to slide inside the 5- inch piping. But each of these five sections of 4-inch pipe also needed additional special piping inside grouped together to include (a) two ½ inch inside diameter tubes attached next to each other and (b) a 3-inch diameter pipe for later instrument insertions. These three tubes needed to be stuck to each other in the same relative positions for each 4-foot section, but all of them could be moved within the 4-foot section to the best place for the instrument pipe to be located, as determined later when all sections are assembled. All other sections could also be moved if needed to line them up with each 4-foot length of pipe.

Finally, he would need a 4-inch diameter "head" to screw onto the first 4-foot section of 4" diameter pipe. That "head" needed to be at least 12 inches long with a 10-inch-long open slot one-fourth of the circumference around the pipe. That "head" needed to have a male end at the rear and then close down to a point at the front end away from the screw threads. He would need these materials by the end of January. The designer said they could have this done by February 1st if he could sign the contract today and pay a deposit of $10,000 toward the total cost of $25,000 because thin-walled PVC was expensive, like everything else in 2022. Dave signed the contract and wrote a company check for the deposit. Dave thought the project really only needed 16 feet total length of each size of piping, but he didn't want to be short, so he got an extra section to have on hand should it be needed.

Dave also called the Central Virginia Tent Company on Pantops Mountain to set up a meeting the next day for some tent rentals starting in February. He then called Dr. Bernstein's office to set up another meeting with him, but his secretary said he was busy with exams, so she took a message and would have him call Dave as soon as possible. Dave gave out his personal phone number for that call.

Dr. Bernstein called back later that evening and said, "Hello, Dave, I'm sorry to call so late, but our exam schedule is underway, and my daytime hours are pretty busy."

"I certainly understand, Dr. Bernstein, and I really appreciate your calling me back so soon," said Dave.

"Call me Sol, please, Dave, since we are working on the same project."

"Fine, Sol, I was calling to see if there is a time for another meeting in your office after exams but before you leave the office for Christmas break. I want to go over some of the details about our drilling techniques and equipment."

"Well, my last day here before Christmas break is Friday, the 16th. How does Thursday look for you, say at 11 am?"

"That will be fine with me, thanks. I will see you then!" said Dave, and he hung up, thinking that the next call would be to Lucy. But he thought he would wait a day or two. Dave's thoughts then drifted to a Christmas gift for Lucy, but he didn't know her address or if he had overdone it at their last luncheon. He rationalized that a Christmas gift would take this relationship into a whole new area, and maybe she, or even he, wasn't ready for that. While he was musing about all those iterations and psychological stuff between men and women, there was a knock at his door.

When he opened the front door, there was a County Sherriff's cruiser outside and a uniformed officer standing at the threshold.

"Yes," Dave replied, frowning.

"Mr. Hutchinson, my name is Deputy Morgan with the Albemarle County Sherriff's office. I have been instructed to place this subpoena into your hands," the officer said, pushing a sealed envelope toward Dave.

"A subpoena, for what?" Dave said, and he accepted the envelope without thinking. "Who is suing me?" Dave continued trying to comprehend what was happening.

"I'm just the messenger, Mr. Hutchinson. You will have to get those answers from your attorney if you have one. Good day, sir." And Deputy Morgan walked back to his cruiser and left.

Unbelievable, thought Dave, what the hell is this now? He opened the envelope and read some of the subpoenas. It was an ex parte motion signed by the Clerk of Court for the Federal District Court in Richmond saying he needed to appear before a hearing on

January 13, 2023, at 10 am in Court 3 of the Federal Courthouse in Richmond. The hearing appeared to be ordered under the Affidavit of one Special Agent Ronald Davidson of NSA under the authority of the President's Executive Order number 22-741A. Holy hell, thought Dave, that SOB Davidson is trying to make the wire transfers a federal case after all.

He called Roger Pettit on a burner cell phone and told him what happened. Roger was incensed and said to bring the subpoena to his office right away. Dave did as he was instructed, and after Roger read the subpoena, he put it down and said,

"I will take care of this, Dave; don't you worry or do anything differently until you hear further from me. The timing of this thing stinks and makes it even more ridiculous. Davidson must have known the courthouse closes down for the holidays and judges are away, so it would limit our ability to find out what this is all about and try to combat it."

"Well, it's about the wire transfers from the Swiss bank account to me," said Dave, "He thinks they are part of some Russian diversion of funds."

"What an insane waste of taxpayer money to be going after American citizens and their lawful businesses. I'll put a stop to this. I know Judge Wilson at that court, and I will talk to him first thing after he returns to the bench and get this subpoena quashed and the NSA off your ass."

"Thanks, Roger, oh, and Merry Christmas."

"Merry Christmas to you, Dave. Let's hope for success in the New Year."

Yeah, right, some Christmas this is going to be, Dave thought depressingly as he drove home. Got the feds to deal with, the project is still up in the air, and life sucks right now. Retirement was supposed to be a time of relaxation. Hell, it was easier working full-time and playing golf, he said to himself. He had just fixed himself a drink and was ready to mope some more when his regular cell phone lit up and rang. He smiled because it was Lucy.

"Hi, there, Dave, it's Lucy," she said, "I hope I am not interrupting your afternoon."

"Hey, Lucy, good to hear from you. I wasn't doing anything important other than waiting for your call," Dave said in jest.

"Yeah, right, and you don't have any hobbies. I've heard that excuse before," said Lucy joking right back with him. "I was doing my Christmas cards today and realized I don't have an address for you for your card, so can you tell me your address?"

"Why, that's very nice of you, but I don't need a Christmas card from you. Just hearing you say Merry Christmas will be enough."

"Dave Hutchinson, don't you take my Christmas joy away from me, you hear, now shut up and give me your address," Lucy said forcefully.

Dave gave her the address and said, "I haven't sent out Christmas cards in years. I usually call friends rather than send cards."

"Well, I didn't send them out in 2020 due to what was happening in my life, and only a few to the family last year. But I swore I would get on with living this year, and that means Christmas cards for me."

"I'm glad you called. I wanted to see if you'd like to have another lunch in Short Pump on Thursday, December 15th. I will be in Richmond for another meeting that morning."

"Oh, damn, Dave, I'm already booked for that day with my daughter and granddaughter. We're headed to the American Girl store in Tyson's Corner for a girls' day out shopping. Is there any other time you are headed this way before Christmas? I would really like to see you again," Lucy said apologetically.

"No, I think this will be it for trips to Richmond until after the holidays."

"Well, I am bringing my mother down here for Christmas and having my daughter's family over for dinner on Christmas Day. If you are not engaged elsewhere, you are welcome to come here for Christmas dinner."

"Oh, wow, that is a very generous offer, Lucy. It's very tempting, and I wish I could accept it. But I had planned to stay here and get together with Richard and another bachelor friend like we did last year. When will you bring your mother back to Charlottesville? I would like to see you then if possible." Dave said with hope in his voice.

"She wants to get back there on Tuesday the 27th because she has a doctor's appointment the next. I plan to stay overnight one night and go with her to the doctor's appointment, but I can do lunch on the 27th if that suits your schedule."

"Tuesday the 27th will be fine with me," Dave said, "Let's meet at Timberlake's Drug Store in their café at the back of the store. It's always been one of my favorite sandwich places. Is 1 pm OK with you? That way, the café should be less crowded."

"I will miss you for Christmas dinner, but I have our next lunch on my calendar now. Merry Christmas, Dave," with a lilt in her voice.

"Merry Christmas to you, Lucy," Dave replied sincerely.

Dave tried to focus on the project but was bummed out that he would have to wait until after Christmas to see Lucy again. *What does this mean,* he thought, Lucy is getting into his heart again, and his head is not cooperating, just like Jefferson's famous dialogue in one of his letters. Dave thought back to their high school dating days and the excitement that weekends provided for social interaction either as a couple or with others at school "sock-hops" after Friday night basketball games once a month. Those school events were pretty harmless and Lucy's parents had a strict 11 pm curfew for her to be home even on weekends. Dave was just starting to revisit their private time together when his burner phone lit up with a text from Chuck,

"Merry Christmas from Maker's Mark and me."

Dave texted back,

"Merry Christmas, Chuck."

And with that mood interruption, Dave decided that sleep was the best alternative for people alone at holiday times.

The next day, Dave went by the Central Virginia Tent office for his scheduled appointment there and laid out his plan for one 10 x 10 tent inside the fence line at the graveyard and the needed canvas screening from the rough drawing he gave them. They had all the equipment on hand and were willing to install all of it and take it all down with 48 hours' notice. Dave said the installation would likely be on January 30, 2023, but the removal might not be until the middle of March. They settled on their standard fee for an eight-week rental, with a 50% deposit and the rest after removal. A bonus payment of 25% of the final total fees was part of the deal for signing the VSRC confidentiality and non-disclosure agreement, and no disclosure was traceable to them. Dave wrote them a check from the VSRC account.

He spent the next few days preparing the drilling plan and making a few drawings to help for his upcoming meeting with Dr. Bernstein, Sol, in Richmond.

Dave arrived at Dr. Bernstein's office at 11 am on December 15, 2022. Sol was finishing up a phone call and then had Dave brought into his office.

They shook hands, and Dave said, "Thanks for seeing me during this busy time for you."

"Glad to do it, Dave. What's on your mind today?" asked Sol.

"I wanted to give you some idea of our drilling plan and then talk about the dental tools and access to the jawline for a tooth extraction," said Dave. "We will start with a pilot hole from inside the graveyard, moving forward on a carefully calculated azimuth and depth. We will then gradually open it up to a six-inch diameter hole using a drilling fluid mixture under high pressure. We will continually install a five-inch support pipe as we go to avoid redrilling. Once we reach the predicted area of the coffin and begin to pick up the wood fiber in the drill residue, we will switch over to dry drilling using an electric blade drilling process with frequent vacuuming. We may even 'feel' a slight break into the inside of the coffin, depending on how much wood fiber is still in board form. I don't know what is inside a 200-year-old wood coffin, but we are expecting some silt that has come in from the decayed top and some other debris, and hopefully not a lot of actual compacted dirt. But, at any rate, we will continue to vacuum and scrape our way to just past the right jawbone. We will then back off the support pipe that we pushed in as we went and inserted a smaller four-inch pipe for our final debris removal to expose the upper right teeth of the skeleton.

As you can see from this schematic," he said as he put the drawings in front of Sol, "this new four-inch diameter pipe will have special compartments for a light and camera in one of the two one-half-inch tubes. The larger three-inch tube will be for instruments to be inserted for the actual extraction procedure. The head of the four-inch pipe will have a special ten-inch-long slot opening one-quarter of the way around the pipe for actual access to the jaw area. If necessary, we will rotate that pipe and pipe head to have it directly over the right jaw. And if we are off slightly on the location of the drill hole relative to the right jaw, we can bring that pipe back out and move the internal tubes around to give us some small horizontal lateral movement in case we did it."

"Once we are directly over the right jaw, we will use that slot to remove the final two to three inches of any material covering the jaw to have it be completely clear for you and your part of the project. There will be a gas-operated generator on-site to handle our electrical needs during the project, especially for this dry drilling and the dental instruments needed for the tooth extraction. In this three-dimensional drawing I have made," as Dave pointed to that part of his drawings, "You can see that the instruments will need to hinge into this cavity from above it and be able to extend down some extra distance in case we are wrong about where the drilling process has put us relative to the vertical dimension of how far above the right jaw we are. There may also be a need to clamp onto the tooth as you drill it to keep it from falling into the head cavity after severing it from the jaw. I'm not an expert on that, of course, but this is what you will have to work with, and I hope you can make some magic happen."

"Wow," said Sol, "That is some challenge. Let me think about this from a dental standpoint with a view toward instrument capability. I will talk to some dental equipment friends of mine because this is not only micro-surgery but from a good distance away and without the hand of the dentist for pressure. Dave, how far will the control console be away from the end of the instruments in use?"

"Right around fifteen to sixteen feet, Sol, but that is from a rigid end of a pipe. We might need a couple more feet of flexible instrument cables to attach them to the console. Remember that we can go as slow as needed, with constant changes of the particular instrument in use through the three-inch main access pipe. The light and camera will always be there, and the camera will be connected to a video display at all times. Vacuuming can be done independently of any other action. And we need to do this twice, so it could spread over two nights during your spring break. And lastly, we will not do any work during daylight hours to prevent the public from being energized or curious by our presence and the noise factor."

"If we can pull this off, what a story of a lifetime for any person involved, professional or contractor, right Dave?" said Sol with a big smile on his face.

"No doubt about that, Sol, but science is the real winner here in many forms if we can pull this off. Let me know after the holidays if the preliminary drilling plan needs any changes to make your work easier or possible."

"I will be in touch with you, Dave, and Merry Christmas."

"Thank you. Is Merry Christmas to you, if that is permitted," said Dave wondering if he had committed a religious faux pas.

"That's quite alright. Many Jews, like myself, celebrate both Christmas and Hanukkah. I will call you with the dental plan as soon as I can conceive of one that will work under these conditions."

Dave drove back to Charlottesville, wondering if the dental extraction part of this project was going to be its downfall. But that assumes we get a positive result from drilling, which was not a sure thing. Anyway, he settled into his house with some more of CJ Box's *Joe Pickett* books for the Christmas break.

On Friday, December 16th, Roger texted for Dave to call him. Dave then used a burner cell phone and called Roger's office. Roger said he had received an email from Harrison Battle that the Foundation would allow the Association to have two vehicle passes for a 2-month period provided (1) the Association's vehicles would not block the main roadway, (2) the Association would be responsible for any damage to the gravel road on the west side of the graveyard, and (3) that the Foundation would be notified prior to any public announcement of the results of the Association's work inside the graveyard. The email also said that the Association had to provide the Foundation's night security people with the names of all people working there on behalf of the Association on a daily basis and gave an email name and address for the person to whom this information needed to be sent. The email concluded with an admonition that all workers for the Association needed to stay in the vicinity of the graveyard, and anyone who was found outside of that immediate area would be escorted off the property and not allowed back thereafter. Dave was relieved that the Foundation had not put in more constraints, like having one of their people be allowed to view the work being done. Roger agreed that the Foundation's requests were reasonable, and he hoped there would not be any problems with unusual or unexpected visitors or their employees adding some new wrinkles into the situation before vehicles could gain access. Dave indicated time would tell about their sincerity, and he would let Roger know of any disruptions in the plan.

Dave researched spy cameras online and found a model suitable for the project from SpyGearGadgets. On December 19th, he purchased the Pinhole Spy Camera HC 100 because the price was reasonable and it was simple to operate through a computer, plus the recording could be saved on a memory card. Dave decided he would take it to an electric supply house to add the needed length in the feed line. Same-day shipping was also provided so Dave would have it by Christmas.

Christmas is a lonely time for people without a family to be around. But Dave was used to staying out of the way and keeping to himself on holidays. He already knew that Richard Dunleavy was going to be away only for three days prior to Christmas but would be back in town for Christmas Day. He had planned for Richard to come to his house then for cocktails, and they would go to Farmington for dinner. But on Christmas morning, Richard called and said,

"I woke up this morning with a sore throat and slightly elevated temperature. I think I'm going to stay in bed today and take some cold medicine to not let anything develop further. Do you mind if we move our dinner to tomorrow night?"

"Consider it done," said Dave, "And take care of yourself. Old marines don't die; they just fade away."

"I think General MacArthur said that about old Army guys, but it probably extends to marines also. I will see you tomorrow at cocktail time," Richard replied.

On December 26th, Dave called Chuck, and they talked for some time about the project. Chuck expected to be back in Charlottesville on January 5th to rent two houses and two passenger vans for the work crew and security crews to use when the time came for them to arrive. Chuck said he had everyone lined up for the work crew, but he was one guy short on the security team. Chuck said,

"Here is how I see the security team arrangement. There are seven days a week with two twelve-hour shifts each day, so that's fourteen work shifts a week. Since each shift is twelve hours, I figured four days on (which totals forty-eight hours a week) and four days off. In order to accomplish that coverage, I worked out a chart that shows it will require a two-man crew per shift, so eight total security guys."

"With the $1000 a week figure you had given me for a salary, it was very easy to find guys. I used that figure for the night shift guys but only $900 per week for the day shift guys. I don't want to rotate shifts since it's only about ten weeks of work. I have interest from four ex-cops, all of whom took early retirement from the Philadelphia police force when the defund the police movement hit that city. I know two of them personally, and they recruited the other two. The other three are existing security guys, where the company went bust after they lost their two largest customers in a contract dispute. As I said, that leaves us short one guy for the day shift. One of the existing security guys knew where his defunct company got its uniforms, so I paid him some extra cash to order us some uniforms already set up with the usual stuff except for the company name, which I figured was not that important. They even provide fake badges," and Chuck started laughing.

"Chuck, you are too much," said Dave, "That is great stuff. If you are one guy short on the day shift, does it matter if that one guy does not have a license to carry a weapon?"

"Not really," said Chuck, "Why?"

"I have a close friend, retired ex-marine, who I think would take care of business and keep his mouth shut, plus he is local and could help everyone out with where to find stuff and places to go without raising hell in the front of TV cameras."

"Sounds like we have our total security team now if he wants to join the group. Let me know when you sign him up. What size is he?"

"Rich is five-foot-eight, about 155 pounds, still wiry and tough as nails. He was a starting defensive back on our football team. He is still fast, quick, and unafraid of contact. Wait until I text you before ordering another uniform."

"OK, I showed all my guys the confidentiality and non-disclosure agreement they will have to sign on arrival, and they know to bring their bank account information. I'm also going to order some heavy parkas from LL Bean, and I already have some extra-large orange construction vests with reflective stripes for going over all that bulk. I want these guys to be visible all the time. The guys know this is outside work and to bring thermal underwear and heavy boots. And when I get down there next month, I want to go by one of those Camping World, RV, or mobile home dealers and see if they have chemical toilets to rent. I don't like the idea of a spot-a-pot on site, but we need to take care of that business too if you know what I mean."

"I like the way you think, Chuck," said Dave, "Always have."

"Thanks, partner," replied Chuck, "Just looking out for the men."

"I appreciate all the work you have done and will be doing soon, Chuck. Keep up the good work. I showed the forensic dentist the drilling plan we developed last month, and he will let me know what the dental extraction plan will be after the holidays if it can be done at all. I will text you later about Rich."

"Happy new year to us all," said Chuck as he hung up.

When Richard arrived at Dave's house a couple of hours later, he brought Dave a bottle of red wine from the Barboursville Vineyard, Dave's favorite local winery, and said, "Merry Christmas, brother."

Dave said, "You shouldn't have done that, but now that you are here, let's open one of my special bottles of 2019 Octagon Meritage and celebrate."

"I thought you'd never ask," said Richard, "That's special stuff. Hey, remember that *$95 GLASS* of wine we had in Hilton Head at that restaurant for the Heritage Tournament? Was that crazy or what?"

"Sure do, and you were the one to step up and say bring it on, you – the guy who made a living off of low-priced stuff from marine base commissaries."

Dave opened the Octagon bottle and let it breathe for a bit, and said, "while that is maturing some, I have a business proposition for you."

"Well, Christmas comes twice this year. What's the deal?"

"It involves my project, and in order to tell you more about it, you need to sign this confidentiality and non-disclosure agreement," Dave said, sliding the filled-in document over to Richard at the kitchen table.

"You already have my name filled in, but there are no details on what I'm supposed to do or the pay," Rich said, picking up the document.

"All in good time, my friend, and none of this will change our going out to dinner at Farmington," Dave said reassuringly.

"Well, if you are involved and have been involved, it must be OK, so I will sign the paper," and Richard signed on the dotted line.

Dave proceeded to tell Richard the main details of the project and that his role would be as a local security agent for about ten weeks, mostly during the day in a twelve-hour shift, four days on, four days off, to keep people away from the site, keep the premises inside the tents secure and provide a brief, party-line explanations for the work being done if tourists asked. He would be paid $900 per week in a wire transfer to his bank, but he was responsible for FICA and income taxes as an independent contractor. He wouldn't have any living expenses since he already had that covered locally. Dave ended with the bonus arrangement for a successful project.

"Wow, I'm glad I said yes. When does this start?"

"Your part probably starts around the first of February, and I will need your bank information before then," said Dave.

"I will have to let the hospital know that I will not be volunteering for a couple of months starting then, but that should be no problem for them to find another volunteer to do what I do. By the way, what is happening with you and Lucy Carlisle? Did you call her?"

"Yes, I called her, and we have had a couple of lunches in Richmond. In fact, we are having lunch tomorrow here in

Charlottesville. I won't tell you where because I know you will stop by just to see how things are going."

"You're right about that, and she does look terrific." Richard winked twice and then slapped Dave hard on his shoulder. He clapped his hands together and said, "but enough of that, where is that wine you opened?"

Dave texted Chuck that Rich was in and poured the wine. The two friends began the "remember when" stories and finished the bottle in the next hour. They enjoyed a fine dinner at Farmington, and Dave slept well that night due to the wine, dinner, fellowship, and the knowledge he was seeing Lucy again the next day.

Timberlake's café was busier than Dave thought it would be when he arrived. He guessed that shoppers were looking at downtown stores to return things or to get after-Christmas deals, but the café only had one table for two still available in the back corner, which was ideal. Most of the other tables, except for a single, looked like they were about to pay up and leave anyway.

When Lucy arrived at 1 pm sharp, Dave stood up. Lucy came over and said,

"Let's have a Christmas hug, Dave. I like hugs. Do you like hugs?" She said as she hugged him fully.

"Well, I'm certainly not opposed to them, especially like this one," said Dave hugging Lucy back. It felt good. Lucy then sat in the far chair to be able to see out into the café, which left Dave with the view of the back wall, but what the hell, he didn't need to look at anything else but her anyway.

"How was your Christmas?" Lucy asked.

"Fine, Rich and I had dinner last night, and he said to tell you hello," Dave asked, "How was your Christmas and getting your mother back today."

"Great! Santa was good to everyone, and my granddaughter fell asleep right after dinner was finished at 2 pm. Mom fell asleep too, but she takes naps anyway. The drive here this morning was fine. She is walking much better, but the doctor's visit tomorrow will be the real answer."

The waitress was there at the table to take an order, so they quickly ordered chicken salad sandwiches, Dave wanted a diet Coke, and Lucy wanted decaf tea. They might have a dessert later. Then Lucy said,

"Are you on Facebook, Dave?"

"No, I don't think much of any social media because I don't see any value in it. Who wants to know what pair of socks I'm wearing today or see pictures of me in a hot tub?" Dave replied.

"I am on Facebook only for my family and some old high school friends. I posted that we were having 'just lunch' events and today was another one. A few of my old Albemarle girlfriends said 'woo hoo' and things like that, all in good fun."

"Well, please keep our stuff private, please, for both our sakes. The project I am involved in has some real sensitivity to publicity, and I would prefer it if all of our activities now and to come would remain private."

"Ok, but you need to move out of the dark ages some also," Lucy said, smiling as a young man came up to their table and asked Lucy point blank,

"Excuse me for intruding, but are you, Lucy Robinson?" He was wearing a light blue oxford shirt, dark pants, and a burgundy sleeveless puffy vest still unzipped.

"Yes, I am," said Lucy.

"I thought you looked familiar." He spoke. "Mrs. Robinson, I'm Sam Carpenter, and I attended one of your breakout sessions at a press convention in Virginia Beach a few years ago. I enjoyed your talk on 'Why Some News is Better Left Unprinted.' I had just finished my journalism degree at ODU and was working that summer at the *Virginia Pilot*. Your session encouraged me to stay with newspaper reporting, and I am now at the *Daily Progress*. I won't bother you, folks, any longer. I just wanted to say thanks."

Fortunately, Dave did not have to interrupt in case Lucy wanted to introduce him to the young reporter because their food arrived at the same time the young man was finished with his soliloquy. After the young man departed, Dave said,

"So, did you know that young man? And Lucy Carlisle Robinson, is it?"

"No, I don't remember him, and yes, that's me, mentor to journalists," said Lucy laughing, "The funny thing is that convention was my last one in 2015 before retiring."

After they finished lunch, Dave told Lucy that the project would be in full swing after the first of the year and his time would be extremely limited. But he hoped he could stay in touch by phone until the project was over. Then he hoped they could spend more quality time together. As they stood up to leave, she said

"I would like that very much. Now, how about another hug?" she hugged Dave hard, and he hugged back. She whispered, "Stay

131

in touch and remember about our experiment," to which he said, "I will," and she walked out of the café.

Dave then went to Lowe's and bought a Black & Decker shop vac and a portable generator and took them to his house. That night he opened the shop vac box and took out the motor housing and guts of the equipment. The next day he took the shop vac guts to an electric supply house, City Electric Supply, and asked them to replace the current motor with a similar variable-speed motor. He explained he was doing some archeological work and needed to have a vacuum source with a rheostat-controlled motor for varying the amount of vacuum at different times. The store said they could do that, but it would eliminate any warranty he had on the Black & Decker shop vac. Dave said he was not concerned about that, and he wanted to know if they could complete this exchange by the end of January. The store manager said they would be finished in about two weeks, and he would call then for Dave to pick it up.

Dave said he had two more minor projects for City Electric. He got out the spy camera and asked the manager if they could add twenty feet of cable between the camera eye and the connection to the memory card box and computer interface. The manager said that could also be done in a two-week time frame. Then Dave said he needed an LED light source no larger than 3/8" to fit into a ½" tube plus twenty feet of cable to a normal male socket which would be inserted into a regular power strip on site. Again, the manager said that could be done in two weeks, but with all three projects needed by the end of January, they might need all four weeks to complete and test all three jobs. Dave said that would be fine and gave him his personal cell phone number to call when the work was ready to be picked up.

On Friday, December 30th, Dave got a call from Dr. Bernstein, who said,

"Hello, Dave. I have some partially good news. I sent your drawings by fax to a dental equipment friend of mine and asked him whether they had anything that could be adapted to have electrical controls from up to twenty feet away. He said they have a dual instrument control console panel on hand which could be modified, but he wasn't sure about the instruments themselves. The advantage of the dual-control feature would be that two instruments could be monitored independently of each other at the same time. He said he would get with his chief manufacturing engineer about the instruments themselves and call me back, hopefully right after the new year. I told him I would need a standard dentist drill bit, a clamp, and possibly a pair of pliers as the instruments. I also told him the school had a tight equipment budget, so these things could not cost a fortune."

That is very encouraging, Sol," said Dave, "Let me know what he says and if you need any funds from here for this specialty equipment."

"I hope the price is right because I want to buy this equipment for the school and add remote dental work as a small part of the hands-on lab experience for students since this will be ground-breaking stuff."

"Sounds good, Sol, and again let me know if I can be of any help. Happy new year to us all."

"Happy new year to you too, Dave," said Sol.

Chapter Eleven

January 2023

On January 5th, Roger Pettit called Dave shortly before noon and said,

"Are you sitting down, Dave?" And Dave was scared that the project was being halted for some reason.

"Why? Is there bad news, Roger?" said Dave expecting the worst.

"On the contrary, Dave. I have good news. Your subpoena has been quashed, and the hearing on the 13th has been canceled. But the best news is that Judge Wilson wrote a scathing letter to Special Agent Davidson ordering him to cease all further investigations into you and surveillance of you."

"Well, that is indeed good news, Roger. Thanks so much for whatever club you used to get that SOB off my case... meaning Davidson, not the judge, of course. How did you get all this done, if I may ask?"

"At first, Judge Wilson was hesitant and said the President's Executive Order carried a lot of gravitas with it. But I told him that the wire transfers were initiated by me from a foreign bank account set up by a client of mine for the sake of anonymity, and I could personally guarantee the Judge the wires in no way were part of any Russian diversion of funds. The judge said that was all he needed to hear and took care of the rest."

"Congratulations, and again, thanks. I'm sure that Davidson is wondering who the hell he was dealing with here in little ole Charlottesville."

"Ha," laughed Roger, "Maybe so. By the way, Jon Coolidge plans to be here on the 13th, so let's plan for another lunch at Farmington at 1 pm."

"OK, got it, Chuck is due here later today, and we will have some news to report. Have a good day, Roger."

"You too, Dave, bye," and Roger hung up.

Around 4 pm that afternoon, Dave heard a car pull into his driveway. He went out to greet Chuck and was surprised to see him driving a 4-wheel drive Jeep Wrangler. Chuck said he had bought that car recently to get around in northern snow. He decided he would bring it along to move people back and forth if the weather got bad during the drilling sequence. Chuck then pulled out four large plastic bags and said,

"Two bags have the LL Bean parkas that I bought for the security team, and two bags have their uniforms and hats. I want to buy four orange coolers while I'm here, two for water only, one for each shift, and two for coffee, one for each shift. Do you think Richard can be the 're-fill' guy and find a place to get coffee and water each day?"

"Pretty sure he can handle that," said Dave.

"I also want to go by a hunting goods store to get about 2-3 infrared game cameras for the security team to put out onto selected trees and then monitor them. One of my detective friends in New Jersey is going to bring eight body cams, one for each of the security guys to have on his chest just in case we have an intervention and need evidence in some legal disagreement."

"You have been thinking hard about this project since you were last here," said Dave.

"Well, as you taught all of us," said Chuck, "Preparation is 90% of each job, and the other 50% is execution."

"I think you have the math mixed up, but I like the teaching point. What else do you need?"

"We will need one of those restaurant propane heaters for the tent enclosure with the Ditch Witch and drilling crew plus the off-duty security guy and coffee, and I guess a second one as an emergency backup. Do you know any restaurant supply houses nearby which might carry these items?"

"No, but I am having lunch at Farmington with Roger and Jon next week, so I will ask the grill manager where they got their outdoor heaters."

"The last detail I still haven't made up my mind on, and we can discuss it, and that is how to keep everyone in touch within each shift. I first thought about radios, but that means an open frequency along with someone to be listening. Then I thought about walkie-talkies, but that's more weight to carry around, so I'm really down to burner phones with just everyone's number for their burner phone in the directory. Any ideas?"

"Not really," said Dave, "I think the burner phones may be the best answer."

"Well, we still have time for more thinking, so where's that drink, and then let's get dinner. I skipped lunch to get here before the traffic rush in Charlottesville," said Chuck smiling sarcastically at Dave.

"Drinks coming up," said Dave, "my apologies. While you are doing your thing tomorrow, I will research rental houses unless you have already scoped that out."

136

"No, I haven't done that yet because I thought that was better left as on-site work as part of this trip," replied Chuck.

The next couple of days were taken up with individual tasks by both Dave and Chuck. Dave also checked into renting two 6-passenger vans from Jim Price Chevrolet, his car dealership, to ferry everyone to and from the work site. On Saturday, January 7th, Sol Bernstein called Dave and said,

"Hello, Dave. I heard back from my dental equipment guy. He said their engineers thought they could rig up something for us, but it would take three months, including some on-site testing. I told him we didn't have three months and asked if there was any other way to shorten the time period. He said they could elevate the priority to emergency work, which would include overtime if we were willing to pay a 50% premium over their base work for custom equipment. I asked him how much for an all-in price to have it ready by March 5th, and he said it would be $45,000, including the console modifications. I gave him the go-ahead as a purchase for my school and said that I wanted to test the equipment on their site when it was ready. I also said if the equipment is not ready by March 7th, they will lose "$10,000 off the contract total as a penalty, to which they agreed."

"Sol, that is fantastic, and let's hope for the best here," said Dave. "The project can help fund this premium if your school needs help with justifying that part of the expense. Where is this company located?"

"Their production plant is in Lexington, KY," replied Sol, "And I asked them to fax their final drawings to Roger and to me before they start production. They will need our approval, and I told them we could do that within 24 hours from receipt of the drawings. I want to make sure we have all the flexibility built in that we might need once we can view the jaw line. It won't do any good then to say we wish we had this or that capability."

"OK, that all sounds great. When you hear that they are ready for your on-site test, I will drive you to Lexington, KY, for that test. If successful, then we can bring all that custom equipment back in my SUV from there to the job site. That way, we can speed up delivery and not have any damage occur. I assume there will be a fairly long umbilical of wiring to coil up and put in the trunk, and the console can ride on the back seat. That will leave us a minimum of space for our own personal overnight stuff. Did this guy give you any indication of how this equipment will work?"

"Somewhat, he said the wiring would be wrapped in Neoprene rubber to not exceed three inches in outside diameter, and their metal head will be similar to the pipe head in that it will have a ten-inch-long slot on both sides of the head. In the head would be three instruments, each one with a four-inch-long shaft that could be hinged down or up through the slot and then extended another three inches on its' own slide bar with a catch button to lock it in place. The actual head of each instrument would be about a half-inch long with a swivel joint that was controlled by the console to activate it in any direction, plus a start switch for the drill similar to how a dentist drill starts now, plus a clamp with Teflon pads to hold onto something. Even fully extended, the instruments can be levered back into the head for removal back out the three-inch pipe. It sounds very sophisticated and one-of-a-kind, but we will be making history, Dave."

On Sunday, when Chuck was due to leave, Richard came by, and they held an "exit update meeting" that morning at Dave's house. Richard tried on a uniform and a parka and found the ones he liked. Chuck got all of his tasks completed, so all the equipment except for heaters was accounted for, and Dave was in charge of

138

heater rental or purchase. Richard said he knew of a restaurant in his area that shut down during Covid and, after re-opening last year, had not re-opened their outside patio. Maybe they had used heaters to sell or rent, but he would check that out. Rich was a scrounger from way back as a marine, thought Dave, he surely knew how to adapt and overcome. Dave also asked Rich to get twenty feet of two-inch diameter rubber hosing to extend the shop vac hose all the way into the area ahead of the dry drill to help clean out the debris there.

Dave said, "The rental house idea looks bleak because most of them had king or queen beds and were not geared up for all males with twins or doubles and the possibility of 'hot bunks.' I looked into Holiday Inn Express and found they had an attractive corporate rate that I could get with our fake company (VSRC) to qualify for it. I first thought about splitting up the crews to different hotels but decided that the bonus payment for secrecy success should be enough to keep these guys from talking in town even when they went out together. So, I decided to rent six rooms for the seven security guys and four drilling crew members plus Chuck at the Holiday Inn Express at the 5th Street exit on I-64 since it was the nearest one to the graveyard at Monticello and also near some fast-food places and not near downtown for walking around there."

Chuck said, "I think that might work out best in the long run since none of the guys were big into cooking at a house kitchen anyway."

Dave said, "The hotel had a free breakfast for the day shift guys, and the night shift guys could go to the hotel breakfast after getting off or to the nearby Starbucks for any kind of food they wanted then. Other than housing, the guys were on their own from a money standpoint, so the hotel route would allow them to keep their food costs down."

139

Chuck then came up with the idea to pair up the security guys with one guy on the day shift and one guy on the night shift in each room to allow each person to have a room to themselves almost. He would pair up with the odd night shift guy since one of the detectives coming as a security guy was a friend who was used to night work before the defund the police movement hit Philadelphia. Dave concluded the "exit update meeting" by saying he would buy a bunch of burner cell phones from Walmart before the security team arrived in a few weeks.

Chuck left mid-afternoon on Sunday, saying he would be back with the security guys in three weeks on January 30th. Richard couldn't stay or go out for dinner with Dave because he had other plans with his lady friend in town. Dave confirmed the six rooms at the Holiday Inn Express on Monday and had them all start on January 30th, even though not all the rooms would be filled that first night.

All of these recent project efforts gave Dave plenty of news to relay to Roger and Jon when they met next at Farmington on January 13th. As Dave left his house and headed to Farmington for that lunch update, he noticed a blue Volkswagen Jetta pulled out of the Bellair Exxon station and got behind him after two other cars. Damn, Dave thought, it's starting again, that guy must either be a new tail guy for Special Agent Davidson or someone else who took down his license plate number and traced it to know his name and address. As Dave went by the entrance to Birdwood Golf Club, he thought about pulling into there and going to the Birdwood Grill and wait there. But if anyone followed him, there was only one way in and one way out, so he would be the trapped guy, not the tailer. So, he kept on going past Farmington and made the same decision about turning into Boar's Head Inn. One of the other cars did turn into Boar's Head Inn, but Dave kept going straight, now with fewer cars in tow. He decided to turn right after the Northridge medical buildings to head to the Ivy Nursery, where he might hide out for a while and see what the blue Volkswagen Jetta did. Sure enough, the last "other" car stayed straight on US 250. When Dave turned right to access the Nursery, the Jetta slowed down but then decided to continue straight also. Dave went into the Nursery and called the Farmington Grill to let Roger and Jon know that he would be 30 minutes late due to being tailed again.

After 15 minutes, Dave left the Nursery and returned to the Farmington entrance without any blue Volkswagen Jetta following him. He related all the new tailings to Roger.

Jon was annoyed by the tailing news and said, "I believe we should move the next lunch to somewhere else because people could easily follow them, even into Farmington's private property, since there was no guard shack at the entrance to check the status of those entering the premises."

Dave added, "I think we should have a code for using locations in the future based on the President of the US's number equal to a letter number where the letter is the first letter in the restaurant name. I think we will need only one or two more luncheon updates in the next two months, so Chick-fil-A restaurant would be a good alternative for the next lunch, meaning that it would be the Jefferson Plan (3rd President = 3rd letter), or we could just meet at Roger's office, but that could lead to the direct involvement of Roger's firm in the project and the press and/or TV outside his office."

Dave then gave Roger and Jon a complete update on staffing, preparations, and when he expected drilling to start. "We are going to go slow all the time and get soil samples each night of drilling and have them analyzed by Southern States Coop because soil tests take some time to perform due to having to send the liquid slurry through successively smaller micron filters and collect the fines of the cloth filters to add to the screened soil for the best results of the actual soil composition. Chuck has been able to get daily turnaround analyses for the project samples from the Albemarle County Southern States Coop, but neither of us wants to overshoot the mark by just looking at wood fiber content in the soil from the decayed coffin. So, we are going to rent a GPR machine for six weeks, which I believe is more than enough time for a rental, even adding in some down time for weather. Even though the GPR will not have specialized cemetery software or someone with the Topographix experience interpreting the disturbances, it will still pick up the piping being pushed into place as the drilling progressed, and that could be plotted against the data on the master cemetery survey chart."

"Do you have someone to film the rest of the project?" Dave asked Roger.

Roger replied, "I have a young paralegal by the name of Brock Fairchild who has been given that responsibility."

Dave said, "Have him be ready to start filming on the night of February 1st, subject to a later text I will send you confirming that date or revising it. Also, give him a short letter on your firm's stationery to verify his identity and to meet Chuck and the night drilling crew in the parking lot of the Holiday Inn Express on 5th Street at 6:30 pm on the start date to ride with them since vehicle passes are limited. Chuck will check Fairchild's ID after producing the law firm's letter."

Roger and Jon seemed very pleased with the professional approach by Dave and his team, so Jon concluded the lunch by saying,

Jon concluded, "I couldn't be happier with the way you have organized this project, Dave. I don't think I need to be back here until you run into a problem or you say we are near to the skull to bring in Dr. Bernstein. I do want to see the actual tooth extraction for myself unless you think I would be in the way."

"Not at all," said Dave, "it would be a pleasure for you to be here with all of us when that momentous time arrives. I will text you using the new code for that lunch meeting. Suppose we also add to the code that the actual day for the lunch is one day earlier than the date indicated in the text and the actual time is 1.5 hours after the time indicated in the text."

"Got it." said Jon, "I will be able to be here with one day's notice," and the three of them walked out of the Farmington Grill. Since that was about all the preparations the project needed until the security crew arrived at the end of the month, Dave decided it was time to call Lucy and stay in touch. He used his regular cell phone and called her.

"Well, hello, project manager. Nice to hear from you," said Lucy when answering her phone.

"Hi, there, Lucy. I'm checking in and staying in touch like you said to do. But I also missed our lunches too," Dave said, trying not to sound lonely, which he was, "How is your mother doing?"

"She is coming along really well now." replied Lucy, "I was with her at her doctor's appointment at the end of last month, and her doctor was pleased with her progress, and the physical therapist reports indicate that those sessions could be reduced to 2 per week in January and that has happened. She has increased the use of her left hand, so all is well for now; thanks for asking. Are you headed this way any time soon for another just lunch?"

"I truly wish I was, but the project is getting ready to start its most intense time in another week, so I will be stuck here, I'm afraid."

"I am coming up to Charlottesville the first week in February to attend my mother's next doctor's appointment. Is there any time then for us…" and Lucy's voice trailed off.

"Oh Lucy, nothing could prevent me from seeing you again except that will be the high point of the project work then. I know that sounds lame, but I ask you to please be patient. If all goes according to plan, I will have some time by the middle of March, and we can do lunch and more then."

"I will hold you to both parts of that promise, Dave Hutchinson. And you stay in touch until then, as best you can, OK?"

"I will stay in touch, Lucy. Bye for now." Dave hung up and thought that was painful, and this project better not screw things up for me with Lucy.

Dave called the Central Virginia Tent Company and asked if they could postpone the tent installation one day to Tuesday, January 31st, and they said that would be fine with them. He would meet them at the Monticello visitor center at 9 am that day. Dave then went to Camping World to buy two folding tables and six umbrella-style camp chairs. He picked up ten chemical toilets on a rent-and-return basis for extra charges to clean them out and restock their supply with new chemicals. They even had a full-size toilet seat for purchase and an attachment to each chemical toilet as needed, so he bought one of those. By now, he had quite a stockpile of supplies at his house to take to the work site when the tent and canvas shielding were up.

By mid-afternoon on January 30th, Chuck texted Dave that the security team had arrived in three cars and were checking into the six rooms at the Holiday Inn Express on 5th Street, so Dave headed over to greet them, bringing their parkas and uniforms with him. As he pulled into the parking lot and over by Chuck's Jeep Wrangler,

Chuck and another guy walked out of the hotel, and Chuck greeted Dave,

"Hello, general, reporting for duty with seven conscripts," said Chuck while saluting Dave.

"Glad to see you back and everyone here safely," said Dave.

"Most everyone has taken their gear in, but let me introduce you to Larry," Chuck said, "Larry, this is Dave Hutchinson, our head honcho, and project manager, and Dave, this is Larry Navarro, a good friend of mine from the great state of New Jersey, lately from the Philadelphia police force." Dave and Larry shook hands and exchanged pleasantries.

"Chuck, if you and Larry have a few minutes now, why don't we go back out to the Chevy car dealership and rent the two passenger vans we have on reserve? You two can drive them back here."

"OK, let me tell one of the other guys in the hotel where we are going. I'll be right back," said Chuck.

Dave drove Chuck and Larry out to Jim Price's Chevy dealership and signed the papers for two 6-passenger vans with them as the primary drivers. He told Chuck that the tent company would be installing the tents and canvas shields the next day at 9 am, so have the first of the day shift security guys ready to go and bring them over to the work site at 8 am. "Here is one vehicle pass, and I will meet you there then, and we will go over the ground rules and pre-game pep talk, OK?"

"See you in the morning, coach," said Chuck.

"There is a Food Lion grocery store, just across from the Hardee's on 5th Street and a Wegman's premium grocery on top of the hill just up from Hardees' and a Krispy Kreme is there also, just don't let them all go into any one place at the same time and terrorize the neighborhood. Let's stay unnoticed, if you know what I mean," cautioned Dave, hoping they had done the right thing by bringing in the security guys from out of town. He hoped they didn't end up being the shock troops instead. "See you tomorrow," Dave said as he left Chuck and Larry at the Chevy dealer.

Tuesday, January 31st, was a decent winter day for Charlottesville, meaning that the temperature was going to be a high of 42 degrees and mostly sunny. At 8 am that morning, Dave met the two day-shift security guys Chuck had brought with him to the graveyard, one of whom was Richard, and they looked official in their uniforms. Dave went over the ground rules for day shift security in that they would have to deal with questions from the public.

Dave greeted the new day shift guy and Richard and said, "you should always be polite and tell them that you are just the hired security guy and you really don't know what the project is all about inside the shielded tent area. Under no circumstances is anyone, even someone from the Foundation staff, to be allowed to go inside the west gate without my written authorization. I have brought a combination lock for that gate, and the first combination will be 2489, which will change once a day at least or maybe even once every shift, which I will discuss between Chuck and myself when needed. You are to work one hour on and one hour off, and your comfort items like coffee and a chemical toilet will be inside. Help me unload my truck with the tables, chairs, and toilets, but put them behind the van for the time being until the tent shielding canvas has been put up. I will be back with the tent people, and then I will unlock the gate. Hopefully, no one will be coming by to visit the graveyard this early today."

Dave drove the pickup truck over to the visitor center to await the arrival of the tent folks from Central Virginia Tenting. He parked his truck in the visitor parking lot there and took the second vehicle pass with him. Around 9:10 am, the tent people showed up at the visitor center, and Dave got into their truck and showed them how to access the roadway around Monticello to the graveyard site. They parked next to Chuck's van on the west side parking area, and Dave went and unlocked the west gate. The tent crew then started with the twenty-foot canvas section on the south fence line from the Southwest corner toward the Jefferson obelisk. They had just finished that section and were hauling the thirty-foot section in several pieces inside the graveyard when a tram bus pulled up, and four seniors got out to visit the graveyard. The tent crew started from the Southwest corner again and came along the west side 20 feet until they got to the gate. They then put up a gate section only and a small section above the gate. They were about finish up with a short eight-foot section beyond the gate, when a couple of the tourists walked around the Southwest corner and approached Dave and asked him what was going to be done in there.

Dave said, "I'm with the tent crew, and we are here just to install some tenting material inside the graveyard. I don't have any idea what the owners plan to do, but as you can see, it will not affect the Jefferson portion of this property."

"Thanks, I was just curious, this is my first visit to Monticello, and this graveyard just completes the trip for me, a lot of graves here. Maybe they are going to clean some of the older ones," the first guy said with a question mark in his voice hoping that Dave would respond. Dave ignored him and watched the tent crew bring in the upright posts first for the other two sides, along with some tent pegs and rope.

The other visitor asked, "Could we just step inside the graveyard, please? I want to take some pictures for my grandkids; I won't take but a minute?"

"No sir, I'm afraid that is not possible, the graveyard is private property, and I don't want to lose my job. I'm sure you understand."

"When I bought my ticket this morning, the agent said this ticket included everything there was to see at Monticello," said the first guy.

"Yes sir," Dave said, "but there are no tickets which will get you *inside* the graveyard unless you are a member of the property owner group that owns this graveyard," with an emphasis on 'inside.'

"You mean the graveyard is not owned by Monticello?" said the second guy.

"The graveyard is not owned by Monticello, you are correct," Dave replied, and a bus tram was pulling up, "and there is your bus to help you continue your tour," Dave waved at the tram driver to let him know the visitors needed to wait for these two guys.

"Come on, Jack. It sure seems fishy that Jefferson's graveyard is not owned by the same people who own his house, let's check this out at the visitor center where your granddaughter works. When she gave us these priority tickets, she said they covered everything we would need for a complete visit."

Fortunately, all four visitors left on the tram bus, and the tent crew finished putting up the rest of the tent shielding material before any other visitors came. The crew then put up the 10 x 10 tent just inside the west gate and finished shortly before lunch. Dave, Chuck, Richard, and Tom, the other day's security guy, put all the gear into the tent area inside the west gate, and then Richard took the first watch outside. Dave had instructed the security team members not to go past the Southwest corner and to simply walk back and forth along the west side past the end of the tent shielding and down to the Southwest corner. Dave locked the gate and made sure Richard and Tom knew the combination to the lock, which should remain locked until the hour when each exchange of personnel would take place. Chuck drove Dave back to the visitor center parking area, where Dave retrieved the pickup truck. Chuck said he would take care of getting the night shift guys there at 7 pm, and Dave said he was going to get two or three bales of straw for putting down inside the tent area to cushion the ground there and keep it dry until the project was completed.

Chapter Twelve

February 2023

On February 1st, Dave got a phone call that the custom pipe order he had placed in December with Charlottesville Materials Company was ready, so he used the pickup truck to get it and delivered all that piping material to the work site by 11 am that morning. He checked all the screw connections, and they all matched up easily. He bought some more bentonite as a lubricant for all piping to slide easily along. He unloaded that along with three bales of straw and asked the day security guys to spread it around the inside of the tented area.

Meanwhile, the drilling crew members arrived, and Chuck met them at the Holiday Inn Express to check into the remaining two rooms the project had rented.

With the tent put up and the screening canvas in place, Dave and Chuck were ready to rent the Ditch Witch JT5 horizontal directional drilling machine from the dealer in Glen Allen, VA. Dave had visited the dealership in January and gone over the confidentiality and non-disclosure agreement with the president of the dealership. The rental was a premium rental with a 25% bonus payment after returning the equipment in satisfactory condition, and no disclosures had occurred traceable to the dealership. Dave indicated he would be there to pick up the Ditch Witch on 48 hours' notice. Dave shared with the president Chuck's background with Comcast in using this equipment, and the crew would all be experienced retired workers familiar with this type of trenching machine.

Dave and Chuck wanted to pick up the Ditch Witch on February 2nd, but there was a light snowfall the night before, so they called the dealership and put it off until late on Monday, February 6th. Dave also let Roger know that the videographer, Brock Fairchild, would not have to start until Monday night. Dave got a call from City Electrical Supply that the shop vac that he had taken there for altering it with a variable speed motor was ready to be picked up along with the spy camera with added cord and the new LED light and cord. Dave picked up everything from that vendor and took that gear, along with the gas generator and a five gallon can of gasoline, to the work site later that afternoon. He also went by the Albemarle County Southern States Coop and picked up soil testing kits plus quart jars for putting in the slurry part of the soil to be tested. He also purchased some small plastic bins for the larger particles of the same soil removed from the screens when the test soil was collected at the work site once each night.

Dave arrived at the work site on the morning of February 2nd with sandwiches as a bonus lunch for the security guys there and Chuck. Richard had brought two propane heaters and the additional vacuum hose for the shop vac. Dave and Chuck went over the plan for Monday, February 6th, when they would go by the Comcast field office in Short Pump to pick up a GPS backpack from there for one-day use, then go to Glen Allen for the rented Ditch Witch machine. Dave would drive his car, and Chuck would drive the pickup truck.

The Ditch Witch dealership in Glen Allen, VA, was open until 5 pm on February 6th, so Dave and Chuck drove their respective vehicles to the trailer rental company near Short Pump, which Dave had lined up for renting a landscaping trailer. They arrived at 2:30 pm, attached the trailer to the pickup truck, and were able to get to the Ditch Witch dealership before 4 pm. The game plan was to load the Ditch Witch and then have Chuck drive the unit back to Charlottesville, staying for two hours in a rest area along I-64 near Charlottesville until 8 pm.

Dave followed Chuck back toward Short Pump, just as a precaution if anything went wrong with the pickup truck or trailer.

151

Then he pulled off and went to the Comcast field office for the GPS backpack to align the Ditch Witch once they unloaded it at the work site. Around 5:30 pm, Chuck pulled into the I-64 rest area near Keswick, VA, and called Dave on his burner cell phone. Dave answered, knowing it was Chuck and said,

"Hello, this is Hugh Hefner's Playboy Bunny House. How may I direct your call?"

"Peter Bilt here, we haul anything, anywhere, anytime. I'm here at the rest home, I mean, the rest stop."

"Good evening, Peter," said Dave playing along, "this is Chester Drawers, and I wanted to open up and let you know I'm going for dinner and will bring something hot with me, so don't fill up on snacks there."

"Roger that, Chester. I'll keep the motor running until you get here."

Dave found a McDonald's at the exit on I-64 at Zion's Crossroads and got both of them adult happy meals with drinks, and continued on I-64 west to the rest area, which required about 20 total minutes from the time Chuck first called. He and Chuck wolfed down the Big Macs and fries and then settled back until time to leave around 8 pm. Dave set his alarm on his phone just in case they fell asleep after such a filling carbohydrate meal and warm car. Chuck wasn't much of a fox-hole talker, so they sat for a while in silence. Then he said,

"Richard tells me that you are seeing a new lady, an old flame from high school days."

"Yep, so far it's been just lunch, but I really like the way it's going, and she seems willing for something more intimate, so you never know at our age, what the tide brings in if you remember the Tom Hanks' line from the movie '*Castaway*.'"

Chuck paused for a minute and then said, "In the cold winter evenings of life, a good woman is hard to beat."

"OK, Confucius, let's move on to something else, or you can go sit in the pickup truck by yourself," replied Dave.

Just before 8 pm, Chuck left the car and started up the pickup truck, and they were underway once again. Meanwhile, the drilling crew had assembled at the graveyard work site around 7 pm and were expecting Chuck and the Ditch Witch to arrive by 9 pm. The drilling team had lots of large battery-operated lanterns to provide enough light for unloading the Ditch Witch. Dave parked his car in one of the parking spaces at Michie Tavern on the way up the mountain to Monticello and got into the pickup truck with Chuck, bringing the GPS backpack with him. They had the other vehicle pass and went to the west side of the graveyard right at 9 pm. After arriving at the work site, Chuck started up the JT5 and backed it off the trailer and then into the graveyard through the west gate. The straw Dave had put down helped avoid any major damage due to the JT5 going back and forth to slowly turn 90 degrees to face the Southwest corner. The drilling crew then departed in their van, and Dave rode with Chuck in the pickup truck down the mountain to his car. Chuck took the pickup and trailer to the Holiday Inn, and Dave went home, leaving the two night-security guys on site.

Dave and Chuck planned to come to the worksite by themselves around mid-morning on the 7th and complete the alignment of the Ditch Witch with the surveying benchmark nails already in place and using the GPS backpack and position rod to guarantee the machine was on the correct azimuth for starting the drilling operation. The actual drilling start would occur later on the evening of the 7th. Dave alerted Roger to have Brock Fairchild at the Holiday

Inn around 6:30 pm on February 7th. That plan worked without a problem, and the actual horizontal drilling started on the evening of February 7th. The goal was to drill only two feet that first night and take two soil samples for testing, to get a base reading on the soil composition just inside the graveyard. Dave took the GPS backpack home with him to return to Short Pump the next day.

The JT5 drilling head had a magnetic transmitter attached to send back exact coordinates to the operator as a steering tool to check on the depth, alignment, and percent of slope. The Topographix map indicated that the skull's right jaw was approximately 3.5 feet below ground level with a margin for error of plus or minus 2 inches. The drilling plan called for a pilot hole to be drilled first with a small drilling pipe that contained drilling fluid at high pressure to cut through the soil and take the drilled material back to a catch basin on the Ditch Witch. That pilot hole then was reamed out on successive passes to a larger hole, finally equaling six inches in diameter. Thereafter, a supporting five-inch diameter pipe was pushed into place using bentonite as a lubricating material and the drilling crew as muscle power. That supporting pipe came in four-foot sections that screwed into the one already in place so that all of them could be extracted after the project was completed. That first night's goal was accomplished by 4 am the next morning, and the drilling team shut everything down and secured the equipment for the next day.

On February 8th, Dave went by the Holiday Inn and left his car there to drive the pickup truck to Short Pump to return the portable GPS unit to the Comcast field office. On the return trip, Dave then would pick up a rented GPR machine the project would need for about the next six weeks. The GPR unit would be suitable to pick up the tip of the metal feed pipe, and Dave could compare it to the GPS azimuth and the cemetery survey done by Topographix last October. Once he dropped off the GPS backpack in Short Pump, he then headed for Reston, VA, for the rented GPR machine from GeoModel, Inc, a leader in GPR use for cemeteries in Virginia. This time he remembered to pack some old blankets and bring some rope.

Dave was back at the work site by 4 pm with the GPR machine, and he and Tom, one of the security guys, got it unloaded quickly. He was going to start it, but Tom said,

"Rich wants to see you before you go; we had a visitor while you were gone. The visitor was not too pleasant and almost got in the west gate before Rich and I escorted him off the premises. Dave went into the graveyard tent and saw Rich sitting and writing out an after-action report. "What's this I hear about a visitor?"

"Yeah, some yo-yo from the *Daily Progress* drove his car onto our parking area from the roadway. As soon as he stepped out, I asked him what he was doing here. He said he was with the *Daily Progress,* and he was here with the permission of the Foundation. I looked at his car dashboard, and he did have a vehicle pass. But I told him it didn't matter if he had their permission; he could only go around the graveyard and not to approach the west gate. He then said he knew you and it would be alright. But I told him, I don't care if you know the Pope, you will not be allowed to go into the graveyard. He then started toward the west gate when Tom pushed aside the canvas slightly at the gate and told the guy he needed to leave or follow the normal visitor protocol of viewing the graveyard from the outside. The guy said the public had a right to know what was going on, and I told the public had no rights inside the graveyard because it was owned by a different organization from the Foundation. He started to move closer to the west gate, but I blocked his path, and we bumped into each other. He said I assaulted him, and that we would hear from his lawyer, but he decided to get back into his car then, and he left in a huff. He drives a blue Volkswagen Jetta, and I took a cell phone picture of the license plate for later use. I checked the game camera on the big tree in the center of the circles, and it has most of the entire incident on video plus, Tom and I downloaded our body cams to flash drives for safekeeping also.

"Well, the only thing I can say," Dave said, "Is semper fi. You guys did a great job. I will pass all this along to Roger Pettit, so if the reporter tries it again, we can get a restraining order against him, or if he is serious about a legal suit, then we have a very strong case to refute any complaints he makes. I'm going to do some initial passes with the GPR machine and then head home. I will see you tomorrow, maybe."

"I'm off tomorrow, but Crazy Brutus works tomorrow along with Little John will be the other day security guy," Rich said.

"How did you guys come up with these names, Crazy Brutus and Little John?"

"They already had those names from the Philadelphia police force. Have you seen John Stenkowski? The guy is huge, 6'8" and about 280, and used to play professional football as a defensive lineman for the Steelers. He suffered a bad double-team block in 1995, which wrecked his knee and career, but he is on his second knee replacement now and doing pretty well. Crazy Brutus tells me that John has some amazing kick-ass stories about the narcotics trade in Philadelphia. Brutus is his real name, Brutus Lucassi. You brought in the A-team, brother. These guys are fun."

Dave started up the GPS unit and made a few passes, then stopped and looked at the azimuth reading and the cemetery survey map. He made one more pass and was finished by just after 6 pm. He called Chuck to report his GPR check on the current drilling progress was right on the money. He asked Chuck to be on the lookout for anyone snooping around at night now that a news guy had tried in the daytime; he is likely to try at night now. The weather report did not sound promising for much progress tonight, so be sure to shut down quickly if it starts snowing.

After only 1 hour of drilling that night, the weather turned ugly with a cold rain that turned into sleet before it hit the ground. Chuck stopped the drilling, secured the equipment, and sent the drilling team to the hotel. He stayed with the night security team to keep them company until midnight, then went to the hotel himself. Before he left, he said,

"Guys, be careful walking around tonight, and don't get injured. There are no replacements. And keep the heater going in the tent so the equipment will not have an oil line freeze up."

There were no incidents during the night nor the next day because the roads were terrible until noon, when the sun briefly came out. Chuck was able to get the day shift security guys to the job site in his Jeep Wrangler, and then he brought the night shift guys back to the hotel. When the sun did come out, it was only for one hour, which meant that hardly much of anything melted. And besides, a low-pressure system was coming up from the southwest over the mountains, which meant a strong possibility of significant snow as it got to the ocean and brought all that moisture back in over central Virginia. By nightfall, that is exactly what happened, and the forecast was for at least ten inches of snow by morning. Dave and Chuck conferred by phone and decided to scrap any drilling that night.

Dave said, "Check on the propane tanks and bring in four more as backup containers to keep the heaters running."

"Right," Chuck replied, "And I will make sure the security teams are switched at 7 pm. I will also make sure that coffee is there along with some sandwiches for the night security crew."

"Let the security guys decide on a reasonable time to be out and be exposed in the expected bad weather. The risk of a visitor is not great with the weather keeping almost everyone locked down for the night."

"Consider it done." Said Chuck, "Have a good evening yourself."

The next day, Dave went by the work site around 3 pm once the roads were cleared by the plows and salted. Chuck was already there and said,

"Do you want to drill tonight? The drilling crew has been off for two days, so working this weekend won't be a bother for them."

"Yeah," Dave replied, "We better get back to business. I hear there might be some more snow next week. I had forgotten what Charlottesville was like in February. Do you want me to take supervision one of those weekend days?"

"No thanks. I like the action, as you know, and I don't like sitting in a hotel room watching TV reruns of Happy Days," Dave said with a smile.

Dave went over to the Monticello visitor center to see if they were selling admission tickets and was surprised to find one attendant on duty. He asked,

"Was a vehicle pass issued to a guy from the *Daily Progress* two days ago? I keep missing him and wanted to find out a name?"

She looked at her computer, punched a few keys, and said, "Yes, a Mr. Sam Carpenter had a vehicle pass issued to him on February 8th."

"Who issued that pass? Just so I can get to them for a contact number for Mr. Carpenter."

"It looks like it was called in by Roberta Carter-Jones."

"Thank you," said Dave, "that will be very helpful." Dave thought to himself that woman was trying to gauge our progress by using the press to do her bidding.

The female attendant said, "I know you will think this is a strange request, but with the snow, we are short-handed, and I haven't had a break all afternoon. I really need to go to the lady's room. Could you stand here for a few minutes, and if someone comes, just tell them I will be back in a few minutes?"

"Sure," said Dave, "I will be happy to give you a break." After she left the area, Dave took out his cell phone and punched up his camera and stepped behind the desk, and took a video screen shot of her computer zooming in all the way to have the permit show up clearly as being issued to Sam Carpenter and authorized by Roberta Carter-Jones. He then stepped back to his original position as the attendant returned to her desk. "Thank you," she said, "I feel much better now." And Dave nodded and said, "So do I."

The drilling team managed another 6 feet of trenching toward the gravesite over the weekend, which Chuck reported to Dave on Monday morning as they were leaving the work site. They really didn't have more than another 3 feet before the cross-over would slow the pace to a crawl once wood fibers showed up in the soil samples. Dave used the rented GPR equipment to plot more progress on the survey map he had been using to track the project. They were right on the correct azimuth and depth based on all the new data from the drill head and the GPR. There was more snow expected Monday, but just a dusting. Even so, Dave told Chuck to give the drilling team the night off and come back on Tuesday to restart that expected last three feet before the cross-over.

Dave and Chuck didn't plan to use a fluid-based drilling process once they were near the actual coffin area to avoid too much drilling fluid saturating the soil around the coffin or skull. Instead, they would switch over to dry drilling at that point using a mechanical router much like the one Roto-Rooter uses for clogged sewer lines. Dry drilling was a much slower process due to blade wear and tear, but Dave and Chuck wanted it that way since great care was needed not to disturb the positioning of the skull. Besides, the Ditch Witch horizontal drilling had been perfect for the precision work which was needed at the start of this project. It was fine with them to switch over and drill some and then vacuum some in alternating passes. The last three feet could take up to two weeks, even with weather delays, because Dr. Bernstein and the custom dental tools were not available until March 5th, when his school's spring break began. The drilling was still on schedule and on target based on mapping and checking the coordinates.

After getting the pickup truck from Richard at the Charlottesville Center on Thursday, February 23rd, Dave went by the job site and picked up the seven chemical toilets that had been used in the last two weeks and planned to take them to the Camping World location in Waynesboro after his lunch with Jon at the Chick-fil-A Restaurant in Barracks Roads Shopping Center. At that luncheon, Dave brought Jon up to date with the drilling progress.

Dave said, "We are close to the cross-over point, which means we will switch over to dry drilling soon. I believe we will complete all the drilling by March 5th, meaning we will be above the right jaw of the skull and have clear access to the molar teeth there. That progress will be visible on our computer screen via the camera inserted into the drilling pipe. If that occurs on schedule, then the tooth extraction will start under the direction of Dr. Bernstein."

Jon was very pleased with Dave's update but said, "I will wait until March 5th to be present for the expected start of the tooth extraction."

After lunch, Dave continued on to Waynesboro to Camping World and exchanged the seven chemical toilets for seven more new ones. He dropped the new ones off at the work site and then went to Richard's apartment to drop off the pick-up truck and make the switch back to his car. Later that afternoon, Dave called Roger on a burner cell phone and updated Roger with the same information that he had just reported to Jon at lunchtime. He also told Roger about the vehicle pass issued to the *Daily Progress* by Roberta Carter-Jones. Roger said he might want to be there when Dr. Bernstein began his work, but he would let Dave know the day before.

Chapter Thirteen

March 2023

By March 1st, the dry drilling and vacuum process had gotten the project to within a few inches past the desired location, meaning directly above the right jaw bone of the skull in the Southwest corner of the Jefferson graveyard. That morning, Dave called Roger on a burner cell phone from the work site and said, "Everything should be ready for having Jon at the work site on Monday night, March 6th. I will reconfirm after getting a dental equipment update from Sol."

The weather had cooperated recently and was expected to remain cold but calm into the first week of March. Dave did some final GPR readings and plotted them on the map being used on-site as a progress map. He smiled at the data and hoped that tonight would show the first signs of the actual skull.

Just as he was about to call Dr. Bernstein, Dave got a call on his personal cell phone from Sol, who said,

"Hello, Dave. I just heard from the Kentucky company manufacturing our custom dental tools. They said they are two days late and want to set up a demonstration visit for us on March 7th. They have been working around the clock on our project for the past two weeks but still have some loose ends to tie up before the 7th."

"Well," Dave said, "I guess in the scheme of things, two days is not a problem for us unless it's a problem for you. As long as these things work the first time at the demonstration visit, then I'm good with it."

"The only problem for me is that it puts a lot more pressure on me for a smooth extraction so that it doesn't extend into the following week when classes resume here at school."

"I understand completely." Dave said, "Why don't you plan to drive here first thing on Monday, March 6th, to my house, where you can leave your car. I will then drive us to Lexington, KY, and I will book us two rooms at a nearby hotel there and even allow for a second night in case there is some final tweaking needed after the demo run. We can get back here even as late as the evening of the 9th and work through the weekend, if necessary, to get you back on your normal schedule. I will text you my address here in Charlottesville to put it into your car's GPS. And keep me posted if there are any further updates from them before the 6th."

"Good plan, Dave. I will let you know immediately if I hear from them again. Let's hope not, and I will see you on the 6th," Sol responded.

Dave hung up and texted Roger on the update that tooth extraction would not begin until the evening of the 8th at the earliest, and that date depended upon the completion of the dental tools being made in Kentucky. He then texted Sol his physical address for Sol's use in getting to Dave's house.

That night, Dave was on hand when the drilling team arrived at 7 pm. He brought Chuck up to date on the dental issue. Dave also said he wanted the drill crew to work continuously now until the right jaw and teeth were fully exposed. He watched the early startup of that night's dry drilling, which was mostly just vacuuming because there was no real compacted soil to drill out at this point inside the old coffin remnants. Chuck had gotten used to the correct knob setting for the variable speed motor on the shop vac, and things were going well. The video display began to show some white areas indicating they were close to the skull itself. Dave thought he ought to stay, but then he also thought he might micro-manage the process too much, and this was Chuck's specialty. So, he bid the crew goodnight and went home.

He tossed and turned in bed that night, wondering if the rest of the evening had gone alright. On March 3rd, he drove to the job site at got there right at 7 am. The security crew was just changing, but the drill crew had already left. Chuck was sitting there filling out a report like he had done for the entire project. Somehow Dave sensed that he should not mess with Chuck by starting with some weird beginning, so he just said, "Good morning, partner. How is everything?"

"Well," said Chuck, "We had an interesting night. Not long after you left, I saw on the video display a movement that might have been the skull shifting, so I immediately stopped the vacuum, and the skull rested back in its original position. So, I geared the vacuum suction down to a lower setting and moved the vacuum tube around to a different area of the open slot. I started vacuuming again, and about two hours later, most of the right jaw became visible. Then, I heard the shop vac motor suddenly whine, and I immediately shut it off. When I looked at the video display, I could see something was blocking the vacuum tube. So, I turned on the vacuum at a low suction power and watched the tube get blocked again, so I pulled back on the tube, which lifted the item up. I pulled the vacuum tube all the way out and looked at what it was," Chuck said, handing Dave a button.

"Unbelievable," said Dave, "This is a whale-bone button probably used as one of the buttons on his shirt at the burial, and somehow it got moved around, and you salvaged a button from 1815."

"Well, I was a nervous wreck at that point and didn't want to tempt fate any more last night, so at midnight, I sent the drilling crew back to the hotel, and I went to a late-night bar for a couple of Maker's Mark drinks and some calming pills."

"You did fine," said Dave after looking at the display screen and seeing most of the right jaw line, "here, you keep the button as a token of your first grave robbery," trying to lighten the mood and stress on Chuck.

"We will go extremely slowly tonight to finish clearing each tooth in the upper right jaw area, I wish we had a brush at this point, but we'll persevere and get this in prime shape by the weekend for the dental extraction to start next week. This is nerve-wracking when you have to do this all remotely."

"Do you want me to be here tonight to have a second pair of eyes?"

"No! I like the action, as you know, and now that I have worked with the sensitivity of the rheostat on the shop vac, I think we can handle anything that comes up. I may want to have a bottle on hand for later this weekend if all goes well tonight."

"Call me if anything comes up, even funny stuff, OK."

"Sure thing, boss. Off to my hotel now, but first, a big breakfast at the Krispy Kreme near there."

On Monday, March 6th, Dr. Sol Bernstein arrived at Dave Hutchinson's house in the Bellair subdivision at 8:30 am for them to head to Lexington, KY, and the custom dental equipment testing for the project. Dave had decided to take I-64 west from Charlottesville, VA, all the way to Lexington, KY, so it would be a long day ahead for them, but Sol said he could drive some of the ways to get them there in one day. They were headed to the

American Dental Supply Company and their EVP of Marketing, Brad Cummins.

As they started west, Sol said, "Brad Cummins is the grandson of one of the founders of Cummins Engines in 1919. His father, Clessie Cummins, was a chauffeur and mechanic for the other founder William Irwin, who was the primary investor in the company. Even though Cummins only had an eighth-grade education, he was an expert on engines, especially for farming operations. The company grew and became noted for its lightweight but heavy-duty engines, but unfortunately, Cummins was forced out of the company in 1955. He kept some patents and began to work for a competitor, the Allison Engine Company, in California. Brad is a 1985 mechanical engineering graduate of Purdue University and has grown through the management ranks at American Dental Supply. I have used several different dental supply companies for purchases at the Medical College, but none of them have the engineering and manufacturing know-how of Americans." Sol then wanted to know about Dave's background.

Since it was a long drive, Dave told Sol the semi-long version of his aversion to design work in engineering school and related his long tenure at Comcast. He mentioned his one hobby was golf, which started a long conversation with Sol about the game and various golf tournaments they both had attended. One tournament, in particular, was the 1981 US Open held a Merion Golf Club outside of Philadelphia. Dave knew all about that tournament because he had a summer job with Comcast between his junior and senior year at Virginia and got one of the Comcast tickets to see the first round on that Thursday. That day, both Arnold Palmer and Gary Player were playing together, so Dave figured that he would follow them until someone else might become more interesting due to playing well. It turned out that Sol was attending the same tournament and also followed the Palmer-Player grouping that day.

Sol was in his final year of dental school at Temple and went to a lecture by another Temple grad about starting up a dental practice. That fellow Temple dentist graduate lived in Wilmington, DE, and was Arnold Palmer's dentist. So, Sol was at that tournament courtesy of that lecturer and even had dinner with Arnold and his dentist friend at Arnold's rented house on the first fairway at Merion. Sol said he tried to take up golf after that event but found it took too much time, which he couldn't spare from his dentist practice at that point.

The two men then talked about the special nature of the Masters Golf Tournament in Augusta, GA, each April (except for a Covid year). Dave had been there on a Comcast ticket in 1997 when Tiger Woods won the first of his five green jackets, and Sol went to the 2019 Masters when Tiger won his fifth green jacket in a remarkable comeback from back injuries and personal issues. They agreed that the Par-3 day on Wednesday there was unlike any other golf event, pure fun with family members as caddies, and the crowd was as close to the golfers as could ever be achieved in a regular tournament. The Masters stories were many and helped to pass the time until they pulled into the Holiday Inn in Lexington, KY, near the American manufacturing plant. They were tired but pleased to be there safely and ready for a late dinner and a good night of rest.

The next day, they arrived at the American Dental Supply manufacturing plant at 9 am and were warmly greeted by Brad Cummins.

"Welcome to America," Brad said, shaking hands with both of them, "good to see you again as always, Sol."

"Thanks, Brad. This is my friend Dave Hutchinson, who is the project manager for our unique event in Charlottesville, VA."

"Based on the length of the umbilical cord for the instruments," Brad countered, "I would say your event is not only unique but historical. Welcome, Dave. I hope our work will receive your highest praise. We have put in a lot of long hours the last two weeks, and my engineering folks tell me they have a great demo to show you. Then Sol can show us his skill in putting the equipment to its full capabilities."

Sol and Dave followed Brad to the engineering department and into a special display room where the equipment had been set up with the umbilical electrical cord reaching out twenty feet through a three-inch PVC pipe through an open window into the next room to an operating table with a dummy skeleton on it. The pipe ended just above the dummy's right jawline.

Brad introduced the American Chief Engineer, Howard Crane, who said he was ready to demonstrate the new equipment. Crane continued, "There are three dental tools at the end of the umbilical cord, a drill, a clamp, and some pliers. Presently, the drill and the clamp are set up to the dual monitoring console, but I will change one of them during the demonstration to then control the pliers later. The first thing I want to demonstrate is the levers on the console, which move each instrument up and down."

Crane levered the drill down to just about touching the right jawline of the dummy skeleton, and then he moved it slightly lower, now actually touching the jawline, and began the drill. He then stopped the drill and moved the clamp down to grasp the drill, explaining that the clamp would now act as the dentist's hand to put more pressure on the drill to make it actually remove material rather than just grind away at the edge without doing any actual drilling. Both Dave and Sol "ooohed" appropriately at this revelation.

Crane then drilled away some fake tooth particles for maximum effect and said, "There was no water cooling in the drill, so some heat might build up with continuous drilling. You should be careful not to drill too long, say no longer than ten seconds at a time."

Then he returned both the drill and the clamp to their original positions and switched the drill controls to wire up the pliers to that console control. He lowered the pliers, opened them with a twist of the control knob, and grabbed the fake tooth, twisting the knob back to secure the pliers to the fake tooth. He then raised the pliers back to the original position, and a fake tooth popped out of the dummy skeleton. The tooth did not have any root canals, figuring that the brittleness of the real thing would break off any root canals still attached to the tooth. A quiet round of applause was given by the assembled group for this extraordinary dexterity for a remote operation.

Then Crane brought out a computer monitor and plugged it into the hub near the console, and said, "This is the real test, having to do this in the dark with only a small light shining and watching the movement on the video display."

Brad said, "OK, Sol, it's your turn to try it out in the dark. There is a second tooth next to the one just extracted."

Sol said, "Well, I don't think it will be as easy as the first tooth extracted, but I will need to do it this way, so let's see what happens."

Brad darkened the room with the dummy skeleton in it by turning off the lights and pulling a shade down on the window between the two rooms. The only light showing up was a small spotlight shining on the jawline. Sol sat down at the video display and moved the drill down to where it was touching the right jawline of the skeleton. He then added the clamp to support the drill and drilled out a small bit of tooth. He then raised both the drill and the clamp up to their original positions and rewired one of the instruments to now control the pliers. He lowered the pliers down to the tooth and, at first, he couldn't get the pliers to open, but soon realized that he needed to turn the knob the other way to open them up slightly. He then grasped the tooth and turned the control knob to close the pliers tightly around the tooth. He raised the pliers up, and a second tooth popped out to the cheers of all assembled in the room. "Wow, just wow," said Sol, "This is really amazing and seemingly so simple."

Dave asked, "I don't want to be a killjoy here, but what can go wrong? And how do we fix it on-site if it does?"

Crane said, "All of this works on regular 110-volt AC power; as long as you have power, all this should work just as you saw. The pliers might apply too much pressure on the brittle tooth and crush it. In that case, Sol will have to decide if the tooth pulp has been damaged or can still be retrieved in a sufficient amount for a legal DNA sample, or he might have to pull another tooth using just the clamp which has a wider grip than the pliers. The clamp might be all you need if the bones are as brittle as you suspect. As long as the three-inch instrument pipe is directly over the right jawline, you should be able to do this operation exactly as you just did it. If the actual location is off to one side or the other, you might have to rotate the instrument head to get the instrument lever down to the jawline on a perpendicular plane. Obviously, if you are short or long, you would just adjust the instrument location relative to the jawline."

Brad said, "Well, does this test meet your specifications, Sol?"

"Absolutely fantastic, Brad," replied Sol, "I already know how we will incorporate this remote equipment into my school's lab experience."

Dave said, "just in case we run into a problem, can we have Howard's cell phone number? We may have to call in the evening because our drilling schedule is limited to nighttime hours only. We expect to do this final extraction tomorrow night starting around 8 pm." Howard wrote down his cell phone number and gave it to Dave. Sol asked Brad to have American send an invoice to him at the school for the balance due on the custom work.

It was 11:30 am when the equipment was loaded into Dave's car, and the two men agreed to get some fast food and start driving. Dave called the Lexington Holiday Inn near American and asked them to cancel the second night he had booked for them. The drive back would take the rest of that day, and they agreed to start on Wednesday night at 8 pm. Dave texted Chuck to get a reservation for Tuesday and Wednesday nights for Dr. Bernstein at the Charlottesville Holiday Inn Express, where the rest of the project crew was staying. He texted they were on their way back now but arriving late tonight. Dave also called Roger and reported the fine success for the equipment testing and asked Roger to have the selected DNA witness be at the Holiday Inn Express on 5th Street at 7:30 pm on Wednesday, along with Jon and anyone else who wanted to witness the tooth extractions that night.

On the drive back to Charlottesville, the conversation was more muted than the drive to Lexington, probably due to the impending historical moment each of them would be facing in the next twenty-four hours. After a particularly long silence, Sol said, "The only thing I am worried about is that the DNA sample might show the skull belongs to a woman, and it does not have any Y-chromosome strands."

"That would be a real downer," said Dave, "I have that fear also. I really want it to be a male and a Jefferson male at that. I have prepared myself that even if it is a Jefferson male, it might not be identical to Eston Hemings' DNA, so some other Jefferson, maybe Thomas himself, still could have fathered that last son of Sally Hemings. I hope we will close the final gap in the scientific knowledge about Jefferson's paternity. I just have this gnawing feeling that Jefferson, at 64, did not father that child. I am nearing that same age, and I like sex as much as anyone, but sex in those days was for the purpose of propagating the human race, not so much for enjoyment and satisfying each other's sexual needs. A lot has been made by the Foundation that Sally Hemings negotiated with Jefferson about her return to America as a slave when she could have stayed in France as a free person. I have a hard time believing that a partially literate girl of 16 negotiated anything with Jefferson. Neither of them is here today or left writings (other than Jefferson saying he did not father any children by her), so I think if a deal was struck at all, it was done by Peter Hemings, Sally's older brother who had been in France all the time with Jefferson. Peter was a trained chef and could stay and have an employable skill, but not Sally. He knew that his chef job at Monticello was secure, and he would have to take care of Sally either in France or in America. Thus, I think he put it to Jefferson that both of them would go back with him to Monticello, provided that Peter would be freed after he trained another Hemings brother to be the chef at Monticello. And for Sally, her children, when she had them, would be freed at 21 or by Jefferson's Will. Sally did not have any employable skills, so Peter probably believed she was better off staying at Monticello and being taken care of by the most lenient of slaveowners until she died there. Neither Peter nor Sally was fluent in French, and of the two choices available to them both, I think that Peter made the decision for both he and Sally. In both cases, Sally needed to be taken care of, and Peter probably felt her best quality of life was in the gentle household work for the Jefferson family at Monticello."

Dave continued like he was testifying as to Jefferson's defense, "I also don't think that Jefferson fathered Madison Hemings either.

172

It's really cruel to think that within days of Jefferson burying his youngest daughter, Maria, in April 1804, who died in the same fashion as Jefferson's beloved wife Martha, two months after childbirth, he would have sex with Sally Hemings with family and friends still at Monticello grieving over Maria's death. We will never know unless the Madison Hemings family relents and allows dental DNA to be collected from the last grandson of Madison, who died in 1940, and tested against all the other DNA now available. However, such a dental DNA sample will never be granted, in my opinion, because the Madison Hemings descendants and the Foundation have everything to lose and nothing to gain by it. The pendulum has swung in favor of oral histories of the Madison Hemings descendants being accepted as fact, and they bear all the risk of having it swing back by more DNA tests."

Dave looked over and saw that Sol had dosed off during his soliloquy, so he sighed and thought to himself that he needed to let go of all these concerns for Jefferson and get ready for what the next few days might bring. He also needed to call Lucy tomorrow after he woke up to check in again and update her that the project was nearing an end one way or the other. Dave pulled into the Charlottesville Holiday Inn Express around midnight and woke up Sol to get him checked in for two nights. He then drove home and took all the dental gear into his house, not trusting this crucial equipment to stay in his unheated car in the coldness of a March night.

On Wednesday, March 8th, Dave woke at 8:30 am, still tired from all the driving done in the last 48 hours. He decided to lounge in bed for another hour but got a text message from Roger Pettit that said,

"Call me ASAP." Dave got a burner cell phone and called Roger.

When Roger got on the line, he said, "I just had a call from Jon Coolidge, and he was not very happy. He said he had been called this morning at 8 am by the publisher of the *Daily Progress*, who said he wanted to confirm a story they were planning to publish in the Thursday edition of the paper that the owners of the graveyard were excavating a section of it looking for the bones of Randolph Jefferson to get a dental DNA sample."

"Oh, no," said Dave.

"Oh no is right," said Roger, "And Jon thinks the leak came from our side. I assured him that I had not talked to anyone, especially a reporter from the paper, and I was pretty sure that you hadn't either. Is that right, Dave?"

"Absolutely right," said Dave, "A reporter tried to visit our work one-day last month right after we started drilling, but I was away at the time, and the security folks kept him from going inside the graveyard. We have video and body cam evidence to show they did this without any discussion of the work or any inappropriate conduct on their part. The reporter's name is Sam Carpenter, and he got a vehicle pass from the visitor center ticket office that day, authorized by Roberta Carter-Jones. I have a photo of their computer record for that permit. She is the source of the leak if there has been one and probably gave up the name of Randolph Jefferson also."

"I will call Harrison Battle in Richmond right now and see if we can stop the publication of this premature story," said Roger, and he hung up.

Roger called Battle, who had not yet arrived in his office, so he left an urgent message for Battle to call him immediately. That return call took place about an hour later, and Battle agreed that it was against the agreement between the Foundation and the Association about the nature of the work being done in the graveyard. Battle said he would call Clayton Lawrence immediately and see if there was a way to stop the publication of this breach of confidentiality. Battle did, in fact, talk to Lawrence about an hour later.

At the Foundation offices, Clayton Lawrence dialed the number for Roberta Carter-Jones and asked her to come to his office as soon as possible. When she arrived, he closed his door and asked, "Do you know a reporter at the *Daily Progress* by the name of Sam Carpenter?"

"I know OF Sam Carpenter," said Carter-Jones, "He used to date a friend of mine. Why are you asking?"

"Because the paper plans to publish an article in Thursday's edition indicating that the Association is excavating part of their graveyard for the remains of Randolph Jefferson. Did you speak to this reporter about that confidential matter?"

"I provided him with a vehicle pass last month because he said he wanted to visit the site and couldn't climb the steps of our bus trams due to a bad hip."

"Did you mention the name, Randolph Jefferson?"

"He asked me who might be in that part of the graveyard, and I said I didn't know but to look up Jefferson's personal letters at the end of 1815."

"You have broken our word by doing all of these actions especially knowing that Carpenter was a reporter. You need to call him and tell him that you are not the confidential source for his article, and if it gets published prematurely from work being completed in the graveyard, then your job is on the line, and you will be terminated."

"You're seriously going to terminate me if a reporter writes something! You can't do that! I will sue this organization for wrongful termination if that happens!"

"I can and I will because you violated a confidential agreement made by this organization, and you were a party to that agreement. You are not the sole protector of our past work on Jefferson's paternity. If new scientific evidence leads people to a different conclusion about our past work, then so be it, and we can respond then as to its validity and relevance to our past work, but not before. Now go call that reporter."

Lawrence then called the publisher of the *Daily Progress* and explained that the Foundation was interested in the work being done by the Association in their graveyard property but that it had a confidentiality agreement with them to not disclose the nature of the work until it was completed. He assured the publisher that the Foundation would be the first to know of the results of the work, and he guaranteed the paper would be the first public body to know the results before any other public disclosure. He asked that the publisher hold up on any article by Carpenter as being premature and perhaps wrong in material respects. The publisher indicated that he wasn't sure what the paper would do with the information known to date, but he would discuss it with Carpenter later that day.

Lawrence then called Harrison Battle and relayed the current position of the Foundation with regard to the publisher and the effect on Carter-Jones if the paper decided to publish an article in spite of all his efforts. Battle then called Roger Pettit to relay all the efforts to keep the article from being published but avoided talking about the possible effect on Carter-Jones. Roger then called Jon Coolidge, who was already at the airport, to take a flight to Charlottesville. He also texted Dave that publication might be held up, hopefully. All these communications took most of the day on Wednesday.

Meanwhile, around 10 am that day, Dave called Lucy, who answered with,

"Well, how is my favorite project manager doing?"

"I'm fine, Lucy, but the project has been hectic lately, but there was a lull before the final big push starting tonight, and I thought of you."

"Well, it's always nice to know that I am right behind the project, Dave," said Lucy sarcastically.

"But you are first in my heart," answered Dave playing along.

"I hope so. We still have unfinished business, you know."

"I am well aware of that promise, truly, I am," said Dave in a more serious tone, "And tonight does start the final push, so in about two weeks, I will have some time to spend it with you."

"So, you are just keeping in touch today?"

"Regrettably, yes," replied Dave, "But the finish line is in sight. If you remain patient with me, we can complete our unfinished business soon and maybe see if there is time and interest in a summer trip together to get away from the daily routine of Central Virginia."

"Well, that sounds wonderful on both ideas, Dave," said Lucy, "What do you see time-wise for the rest of the project?"

"I'm guessing my part will wind up by the end of April."

"Sounds good. Keep in touch, Dave Hutchinson."

"I will certainly do that, Lucy," said Dave, "Bye for now."

Dave called Chuck on a burner phone and told him he would come by the work site around 6:45 pm with the dental equipment in his own car. After unloading it, he would then use the 6-passenger van to drive to the Holiday Inn Express to pick up Dr. Bernstein, Roger, a witness, and Jon, all of whom wanted to see the extraction scheduled for tonight. He asked Chuck to take the night security guys and drilling crew members over to the work site around 6:30 pm and get everything ready for the main event.

At 7:30 pm on Wednesday, March 8th, Dave drove up to the parking area of the Holiday Inn Express and saw a group of people standing at the entrance portico. He got out of the van and shook hands with everyone he already knew, saving Roger for last, who introduced Fred Phillips, one of two partners in the small real estate law firm of Becker and Phillips. Fred was a friend of Roger's who had been signed up to be the independent witness to the dental DNA collection via a remote tooth extraction and delivery to the FBI laboratory in Quantico, VA.

Dave drove the group to the Jefferson graveyard and parked on the west side as usual. Everyone else was already there, including Roger's paralegal, Brock Fairchild, who had been recording everything on the project since the beginning of drilling a month ago. Chuck had all the equipment set up and the generator running. He had set up Dave's laptop computer to be the video display and plugged everything into the hub attached to the computer. Anything that had an electric plug had been connected to the power strip connected to the generator. The LED light and camera had both been inserted into their respective half-inch tubes, and the display showed a right jawline with its upper teeth fully exposed. Those actions had been recorded before the arrival of Dave and his guests, but Chuck decided to leave the insertion of the umbilical instrument grouping to Dr. Bernstein.

Roger broke the tension by saying, "Well, Sol, it looks like you have a reserved seat to make history."

Sol responded, "And I didn't even think to bring my dentist lab coat," which got a chuckle out from everyone present, "And it looks like Dave and Chuck have placed us directly over the right spot as expected. Good work, you guys."

"Thank modern technology like GPS and GPR for precise measurements not available to previous explorers," said Dave.

Chuck said, "As a guide, I have already marked where on the umbilical cord we should stop pushing the instruments in. We can then adjust them based on having the head show up in the video display."

Dave added, "Chuck, why don't you and the drilling crew assist Dr. Bernstein with the insertion of the umbilical instrument grouping."

"Our pleasure," said Chuck. And the team slowly picked up the head and first several feet of the umbilical cord and fed it carefully into the open three-inch tube. Everything fit smoothly, and the mark Chuck had made previously at the sixteen-foot length came up reasonably quickly. The team stopped at that point but didn't see anything on the video display from the camera in its position, just the teeth and jawline. So, the team inched the cord forward another six inches, and there was the first sign of the pointed tip of the headpiece. They moved the line forward another ten inches, and the entire headpiece was now visible with the open sides above and below as needed.

Sol then checked the connections for the drill and the clamp as the first two instruments he would use. He moved the drill lever slightly down, and the drill descended from its starting point to point down toward the jawline. He continued to move the drill down to where it was perpendicular to the jaw line and almost touched Molar Tooth 3. He then decided to raise the drill back up and do the same procedure with the clamp using the other dual control on the console. It responded in the exact same way, and the interested spectators "oohed and ahhed."

Sol said, "I was going to use the drill only first like I did for the demo at the factory, but we were working on a bottom tooth there, and here we're lined up to extract an upper tooth, so I think I will clamp onto the tooth first, as a precaution, and then drill some." He clamped on Molar Tooth 3 and then moved the clamp further down to see if the Molar would break free. There was a small crack, but it didn't free the Molar, so he brought the drill down and drilled at the intersection of the tooth and jawline. Even without the pressure of a dentist's hand, the weight of the drill was enough to remove some jaw material in the first ten seconds of drilling. Sol pulled down on the clamp lever, and the Molar gave way to the cheers of all spectators.

After returning the drill to its original starting position in the headpiece, Sol then raised the clamp to its original position with the tooth still firmly in the clamp. At that point, there was a discussion about turning the umbilical grouping and headpiece ninety degrees to put a closed side under the tooth, but the consensus was that move was just as dangerous to lose the tooth as slowly withdrawing the entire assembly. Chuck and his team pulled very lightly to get the umbilical grouping and headpiece moving backward and sustained that pressure until they had pulled the entire umbilical grouping all the way out. Sol put on sanitary gloves and said,

"Dave, would you lever the clamp control slightly up and out of the headpiece so I can remove the tooth?"

"Sure, Sol," said Dave, and he moved the clamp out of the headpiece and reversed the pressure by turning the control now to open the clamp.

Sol pulled out the tooth and placed it in a plastic evidence bag. He had two pieces of evidence tape laid out, and he wrote his name in the script, plus the date and time, and added his signature. Then he said,

"Mr. Phillips, would you do thing by signing your name to the other piece of evidence tape and dating it?"

"OK. Do you want my full signature?" asked Fred.

"Just your normal check-writing signature will do," replied Sol.

When Fred completed his task, Sol pulled off the backing of his piece of evidence tape and attached half of it to the front of the evidence bag, looping it over the top of the bag to have the other half attached to the back of the bag. Then he said,

"Mr. Phillips, would you now do the same thing with your piece of evidence tape?" Fred did as instructed and attached the evidence tape to the front and back of the bag.

"Now, Mr. Phillips," Sol continued, "Please hold this completed evidence bag while I return to the task at hand to go in for a second tooth."

All the procedures were repeated with the same positive result for the Molar Tooth 2. And when Fred finished with his last step, they had two completed evidence bags. Then, there were cheers all around. Dave was certain that any nearby neighbors probably heard this noise, and he wished he had thought to bring champagne. But Chuck came to the rescue with a bottle of Maker's Mark bourbon and some plastic cups, and everyone toasted the success of the

181

project to produce dental DNA without exhumation. Sol was especially excited to write up this project for one of the dental journals, but Roger asked him to wait until the final DNA results were known and, if successful, a press conference would be held.

Dave returned the visitor group to the Holiday Inn Express. Fred Phillips agreed to pick up Sol there the next morning to drive to the FBI laboratory in Quantico, VA. Dave asked Brock to also go along and record the two men handing over one of the samples. The time of 8:30 am was set for pick up at the Holiday Inn. Sol agreed to keep the second sample unopened with him until the press conference or if there was any problem with the first sample and FBI testing. Dave said he would take care of the dental equipment and get it to his house to put all of it into Sol's car when Sol got back there from the FBI delivery. Roger and Jon were very pleased with the results and congratulated Dave on the success of the project. Dave reminded them of the bonus payment arrangement.

Dave went back to the graveyard site in his own car, where the crew had finished off the bottle of Maker's Mark, of course. Dave said to Chuck,

"Can you and the drilling team guys be ready to load the JT5 horizontal drill machine around 7 pm tomorrow night? I will use the pickup truck and swing by the Holiday Inn Express to attach the trailer before coming to the work site."

"Sure thing." Said Chuck, "We'll be here and ready to load it then."

Dave then said to all the crew, "You guys should come to the work site tomorrow night at 7 pm in the van for a short final celebratory gathering after loading the JT5 machine and disassembling the drill pipes. You can then check out of the hotel Friday morning and head home. By the way, Chuck, are you OK to drive these guys back to the hotel? I don't want any mishaps, now at the end."

Chuck said, "I can handle the driving just fine now."

Dave packed up the dental equipment and console into his car and left the work site to drive home. He felt very tired now from driving and the successful completion of a difficult project. He brought the dental equipment inside his house to avoid leaving it outside in his car on the cold March evening.

The next day, Dave used the pickup truck to return the GPR unit to its owner in Reston, VA. The dental DNA sample was delivered to the FBI lab unopened by Sol Bernstein and Fred Phillips. Both Dave and Sol got back to Dave's house around the same time, shortly before 4 pm. Dave packed all the dental equipment into Sol's car and said, "It's been a pleasure working with you, Sol, and I hope the school enjoys its new role as a visionary for the dental sciences."

"That's very kind of you to say, Dave," said Sol, "And I also enjoyed our collaboration. Take care of yourself." And the two men shook hands, and Sol drove back to Richmond. Dave drove over to the Bellair Exxon for an evening paper and was relieved to see there was no article in it about the project, at least on that Thursday. He texted Roger that the newspaper was "clear." He then went to the Holiday Inn Express and attached the trailer to the pickup truck before going to the work site.

On Thursday night, March 9th, the drilling crew arrived as usual at 7 pm. They loaded the JT5 onto the trailer and disassembled the drill pipes. Dave had brought a catered meal from Foods of All Nations in Charlottesville, one of Dave's favorite sources for take-home meals. The food consisted of fried chicken, a shrimp platter with cocktail sauce, some deviled eggs, and a large number of brownies and chocolate chip cookies. It was a farewell meal, so to speak. Dave told the crew that he appreciated all their help and that it could not have been a successful project without their diligence and hard work. He asked them to remain quiet about their work there for another 60 days because it would take that time for the results to arrive and for the property owner to decide whether or not to make them public. He was confident that the project part of the work had been done well and the promised bonus would be forthcoming, but he asked them to be patient until the publication decision was made. He estimated that all this would become final by early May because that coincided with an annual meeting of the property owners later in May.

"Since you are paid weekly," Dave continued, "I will not take you off the payroll until the weekend. Therefore, you have a nice hourly pay rate for this week, so have a safe journey back to New Jersey tomorrow."

With that, Dave raised his coffee cup and said, "Here's to you guys. You made it happen."

"Here, here," was the refrain from all the guys assembled, and they drank some of their dinner coffee. He told Chuck to get some rest then but leave the night security guys there until morning. Dave said he had called the Central Virginia tent people to come out and have them take down the tenting on Friday morning. He wanted all the security people to come the next morning to help clean up the site after the tent people removed their materials. He would bring a bunch of donuts with him for the morning farewell toast with the security guys.

On Friday morning, all the security guys were assembled at the work site at 7 am, along with the existing two night-security guys coming off duty. Dave gave the same speech given to the drilling guys last night; he now gave it to the combined security guys that morning. Although the security guys didn't have the same spread as the drilling team, Dave had brought two dozen Krispy Kreme donuts for the group and an extra dozen for each guy to take home.

"Whether you make it home with the extra dozen or eat them along the way will be up to you, but thanks for all your hard work," said Dave while toasting them. He gave them the same details about the promised bonus pay as he had given the drilling team the previous night.

"Chuck, will you come back here after you take these guys back to the hotel? They can check out of your rooms except for the two night guys from last night. You two guys can stay in your room one more day and night and check out tomorrow morning. It's up to you, but don't have any accidents heading home because of lack of sleep."

Dave waited at the Visitor Center for the Central Virginia tent people to arrive, which they did at 9:30 am. At the work site, the tent crew made short work of taking down all the tenting materials, and then Chuck returned as expected. Dave had purchased twenty-five pounds of grass seed to replenish what might have been torn up by the work in the Southwest corner of the graveyard. Dave, Chuck, and Richard spread the grass seed quickly on the work site. Fortunately, no visitors to the graveyard showed up, and not even a tram bus came by during this cleanup activity.

"Chuck, would you and Rich return the rented vans to Price Chevrolet? Rich knows the way. I will meet you there in an hour to bring you both back to the Holiday Inn."

Rich said, "I will take the chemical toilets back to Camping World."

"Thanks, Rich," replied Dave.

Dave loaded the tables and chairs into the pickup truck and told Richard to keep them along with the truck. Then Chuck, Richard, and the other day's security guy all left, leaving Dave alone with his thoughts and to look over the graveyard for the last time. Dave did not see any damage to the road or circle on the west side but took cell phone pictures of them anyway. After picking up both Rich and Chuck from Price Chevrolet, Dave drove them back to the Holiday Inn Express on 5th Street. He asked if they had time for a celebration lunch at Wegman's on the hill behind the Holiday Inn. Richard said he had time, but Chuck demurred and said he could miss some DC traffic if he got on the road now. Chuck and Richard shook hands, and Dave walked Chuck over to his Jeep Wrangler.

Dave said, "It has been great, old friend. I couldn't have done this without you."

"Same here, buddy," replied Chuck, "but let's not get all sappy now, and no hugs. Just send that bonus money when you can, that will be the best farewell hug."

They shook hands, and Dave said he would keep in touch in case another project popped up.

Dave and Richard went to Wegman's for lunch. During lunch, he thanked Rich for his work on the project and asked if he was free for dinner on Saturday night. Richard said he was, and it was his pleasure to be a part of the project. Richard said, "I'll come by your house around 5 pm for wine before dinner."

Dave decided to go to Farmington to hit some golf balls. He stayed for dinner at Farmington on Friday night because he felt like celebrating but had no one to do it with, and besides, he was out of his supply of pre-made dinners.

The next day, Dave called Lucy around 11 am, and Lucy answered,

"Hello, stranger. How is the project going?"

"Hi, Lucy, just checking in to stay in touch like I said I would do. My direct part of the project is wrapping up, but there is still some behind-the-scenes work by others before a final conclusion can be made."

"Does that mean you will have more time for lunches now?"

"I think that could definitely be in the cards. Do you want to meet in Short Pump again, or are you coming to Charlottesville soon?"

"Neither. I want you to come here to my house so I can fix you a nice homemade dinner. Are you available this Saturday?"

"It's been a long time since I have had anything homemade, but this weekend is out because I have a thank-you dinner set up with Rich for this Saturday. How about the following Saturday or any time during next week?"

"The Richard dinner sounds like a copout to me, Dave Hutchinson. Are you running around with some sweet young thing in Charlottesville that you don't want me to know about?"

"Lucy, you've got me pegged all wrong. The Richard dinner is real, just call him, and he will verify it. He wouldn't cover for me. Besides, I only have eyes for you like the old song said."

"OK, mister smooth, I'll trust you for a while longer. The following Saturday is fine with me. I will text you the directions to my house next week. Stay in touch."

"Looking forward to it, Lucy, and I'm mister stay in touch. Bye," and Dave hung up.

Dave had a good round of golf on Saturday and took some money from his golfing foursome. The Richard dinner was good too, because the strain of the project was removed from both of them.

That Sunday, Dave did research into DNA testing and began to summarize his findings in writing as he normally did. Sons receive their Y-chromosomes from their fathers without mutation, except in rare situations over thousands of years, and they pass the identical Y-chromosomes onto their sons, so direct lineage can be traced from current males back to parental males many generations ago. Y-chromosome testing consists of short random repeats (STR) of the A, D, T, and G chemicals found in the male Y-chromosome using anywhere from 12 to 111 loci of DNA segments, given the name DYS for short. While 14 DYS loci can be enough testing for families like the Jeffersons, which have a rare genetic DNA chemical composition or only limited amounts of genetic data in the international database, 67 DYS loci testing has become a better indicator of father-son relationships for DNA testing, especially markers 16-28. The test results come in the form of a group of numbers indicating the number of STRs within the number of DYS loci tested, and the group of repeats itself is called a haplotype.

Dr. Bernstein's forwarding letter to the FBI laboratory was for them to test all 67 of the standard DYS loci, but especially markers 16-28, for a father-son DNA analysis because that was the relationship that was expected for "Patient XYZ." Keeping the name of the DNA source anonymous would ensure FBI independence until the final results were known, as was the intention of the Monticello Association from the start. Only Dave, Dr. Bernstein, and a few others knew the possible name of the DNA source at this point. Billing for the work done was set up through Dr. Bernstein,

188

again to avoid indicating who this test was for, either as a patient or requesting group.

That Monday, Dave got a call on his regular cell phone, but he didn't recognize the number calling even though it had a local area code. So, he let the message answer part answer the call. About a minute later, he heard the sound the phone makes when it has a voice message. When pressed the button to play the voice message, it said

"Mr. Hutchinson, this is Sam Carpenter with the *Daily Progress,* and I wanted to talk to you about the work done in the Monticello cemetery. I know you have blocked my previous phone calls, but I really need to speak with you about how roughly I was treated last month when I visited the property. The security officer was very belligerent and rude toward me, and I think I'm owed an apology. I am just trying to do my job to help the public understand work was being done there. Call me back on this number."

This guy Carpenter needs to get into another line of work, Dave thought; he has no clue as to how to approach people. There is no way I'm going to talk to him even if he stops following me.

On Thursday, March 23rd, he got a call from Roger that Dr. Bernstein had finally received the written report on the dental DNA sample sent to the FBI laboratory. The report was for "Patient XYZ" to keep it anonymous until later, and Roger said it showed the genetic data for the haplotype sequence for "Patient XYZ" along with the FBI standard procedures used to achieve the DNA fingerprinting through short tandem repeat (STR) microsatellite haplotype markings and one mini-satellite MSY1 signature. Roger admitted that he didn't know what the FBI report meant at that point because Dr. Bernstein said that the report needed to be given to a board-certified pathologist and then compared with the haplotype sequence for the descendant of Eston Heming who participated in the Foster 1998 DNA study. Roger said the next step was to

189

complete that comparison, and he would take care of that step right after he called Jon Coolidge with an update on the FBI report.

When Dave hung up on the call from Roger, he immediately smiled and thought of the strange coincidence that all of this might be completed by April 13th, which was Thomas Jefferson's birthday. Maybe Mr. Jefferson was speaking from his grave, thought Dave, but only as a passing thought.

Dave got a text message from Lucy with directions to her house and a question

"What do you like to eat?" Dave thought about meatloaf since he had that Banquet prepared version with brown gravy a lot, but he thought that it was too bland for a special home-cooked meal. He discarded any ideas about meat grilling on an outdoor grill because he ought to do that if that was the main meat dish and he hadn't grilled in a long time. He didn't like most fish, except for shrimp. Damn, this was getting more difficult by the minute, he thought. Then he decided to text back to Lucy

"Anything Italian with meat sauce in it or on it." He hoped that gave her enough leeway to do something special in the Italian food line.

On Saturday, March 25th, he arrived at Lucy's house a 5 pm, bringing another one of his bottles of 2019 Octagon Meritage from Barboursville Vineyard. Lucy met him at the front door with an apron on but gave him a big hug anyway.

"I was just finishing up the homemade Caesar dressing for our salad," she said, taking off the apron, "Why don't you open the wine, and we can sit out on the screened-in porch and talk for a while."

"More than happy to take care of that job as sous chef, Mrs. Robinson," Dave said as he started to hum the Simon and Garfunkel song from the old Dustin Hoffman-Anne Bancroft movie.

"Let me guess, you used to do backup vocals for Simon and Garfunkel," Lucy said, smiling.

"They asked me, but I turned them down because I was still in grade school," Dave responded.

They sat down on the porch, which had a nice view of a small stream out back, and Dave complimented Lucy on her house and property and especially how well she looked tonight.

"Are you trying to butter me up to make this the night for the snoring experiment, Dave Hutchinson?"

"No, ma'am, that experiment is reserved for a different time and place," Dave said, but he wished he had just said yes.

The evening at Lucy's house was going great, and her Lasagna was to die for, but then the phone rang. Lucy answered it, and it turned out to be her daughter, who had a question for Lucy concerning the significance of a fever temperature of 101 degrees for her granddaughter. Lucy had to have an extended conversation about what it could be and the next steps. Once that conversation was finished, Lucy said she was sorry for the interruption. Dave said he understood but felt that the interruption was a message that he should call it a night. He got up, even though Lucy wanted him to stay. Lucy's eyes were glistening like she was about to cry, so Dave decided it was time for a kiss. The kiss was warm and long, and both of them seemed to feel a spark had been lit. Dave left before something else could be lit and visible.

Roger Pettit called on the following Monday and said, "I talked to Jon Coolidge over the weekend. I recommended sending the FBI analysis and the Foster haplotype visual contained in the *Nature* publication from November 1998 to Dr. Sanjay Patel, a board-certified pathologist and chief of the pathology laboratory at the University of Virginia. Dr. Patel has agreed to be engaged to compare the two haplotype sequences for "Patient XYZ" and that of the male descendant of Eston Hemings and to evaluate if "Patient XYZ" could be the father of Eston Hemings. Dr. Patel agreed to send his findings and conclusions back to me. He indicated that he would be able to complete the assignment in about a week, so things are closing in on a result one way or the other."

Dave said, "That is great news, and I will be hoping for a favorable result for the Monticello Association. By the way, I need to return a key to you for the west gate entrance at the graveyard."

Roger concluded, "For a favorable result, Jon has already authorized him to set up a press conference for the last week in April 2023. I believe that such a press conference could be a momentous event and that we should engage a professional public relations firm to have this event done right. Bring the key with you the next time we meet here or at Farmington."

Dave wanted to know if Roger needed any help from him, but he didn't know anyone in town with PR experience.

Roger said, "I will likely contact Davis and Mathews in Richmond. They specialize in PR work and have been used in the past by local and state government entities and the Governor himself for important PR press conferences. But that engagement will await the final results from Dr. Patel and the final "go" decision from Jon Coolidge. If there was such a go decision, then you might be needed for a meeting with the PR firm to cover the project details and provide needed narratives for the DVD, which I am having made by a film editing firm from the filming done by my paralegal, Brock Fairchild, who photographed the project's main activities."

Dave then softly reminded Roger that Jon needed to approve the bonus payment money even if the result was not what the Association was expecting because the project was certainly successful from that bonus standpoint. Roger assured Dave there would be no problem with releasing those wire transfers soon.

When Dave hung up from talking to Roger, he had the gnawing feeling that somehow the bonus arrangements were not going to be paid. It wasn't that he didn't trust Roger or Jon, but the project team was now out of the picture and was becoming a fading memory. Hopefully, this would all be settled correctly because Dave didn't want to have to consider another law firm for filing a lawsuit if this bonus money was canceled. He disliked not being in control when projects were done well and something else intervened to screw things up. But he and the team were stuck with letting this play out and he tried to avoid thinking ill of the project originators.

Chapter Fourteen

April 2023

Two weeks later, Roger called Dave and said this was a conference call with Jon Coolidge on the other line also. Jon said hello to everyone, as did Dave, and the air was tense, waiting to hear what Roger had to say. He started by saying he had received the Affidavit from Dr. Patel and that he wanted to read it to Dave and Jon. Rather than just summarizing the ending, Roger dragged it out by starting with Dr. Patel's professional qualifications and then his scientific procedures in comparing the haplotype sequences in the FBI report on "Patient XYZ" attached as Exhibit A to the Affidavit with the haplotype sequence for the descendant of Eston Hemings from the DNA report in the British scientific journal *Nature* in November 1998. Then Roger read the third part about Dr. Patel's success in getting the original test data from the Oxford University database for that 1998 testing, which included 28 markers, but the Foster report had truncated them to just the first 14 because none of the 1998 father-son combinations were identical. Foster did have identical results in those first 14 markers, which showed that the descendant of Eston Hemings and the Jefferson descendants tested were in the same haplotype group, so Eston Hemings was fathered by SOME Jefferson.

Dave kept thinking, why can't he just get to the point when Jon said, "Get to the conclusion, Roger." Roger laughed and then read the final paragraph, "Therefore, it is my professional opinion that the male Y-chromosomes identified by the haplotype sequences in the two attached exhibits are identical in the father-son markers, indicating a direct male lineage for these two individuals, so there is a 99.9% probability that Patient XYZ is a Jefferson and the father of Eston Hemings."

"I'll be damned," said Dave, while Jon said, "that is absolutely incredible. The Association will be very pleased to hear this news next month. Of course, there will be at least one member who will be pissed, but finally, science has prevailed. What's next now, Roger?"

"Well, I would like to engage that Richmond PR firm that I told you about to prepare materials and talking points for a press conference early next month. We will need both of you to be available for that event along with Dr. Bernstein, but I will let the PR company do its thing and tell us how to make this event happen correctly."

"And can we get a resolution on the bonus money, Jon?" Dave said, hoping he didn't step out of line, but the timing couldn't be any better.

"I think we can release those monies now, Roger. I assume Dave can give you the amounts for each person and I will trust that you will make those distributions this week. We can process your firm's billing after the press conference."

"OK, Jon, I think that's fair. Dave, can you give me a list and amounts, say tomorrow morning by email?"

"It will be my pleasure, Roger and Jon. Thank you for such an incredible opportunity to help out in this historic outcome."

Dave was ecstatic and wished someone was there to celebrate with him, especially if that someone was named Lucy, but that would have to wait. The next morning, he emailed Roger with the list of individual and corporate contractors and the bonus amounts.

Roger called him afterward and said the amounts looked reasonable based on when people actually worked, so he would get the wire transfers in motion. He also said that Bruce Mathews would be in his office on Friday, April 14th at 10 am, and it would be good if Dave was there to add some brief details about the project. Dave told Roger he would be there.

Thursday night, Chuck texted Dave on his personal cell phone,

"Call me." Dave was worried that something was wrong, so he used his last burner phone to call Chuck. When Chuck answered, he said

"I didn't have any burner phones left, so I hope I didn't screw up by texting you. I am correct that this is the Devil, right?"

"Yes," said Dave, "And you are scheduled for an arrival next week."

"Well, in that case, I'm going to have one hell of a party and spending spree. I just wanted to thank you for the bonus wire transfer that hit my account last night. I saw it today as I was paying some bills online. You always were a straight shooter with everyone, and it was a pleasure working for you now, just as it was when I worked for you at Comcast."

"Well, that is very kind of you to say, Chuck. The pleasure was and has been all mine."

"By the way, I got calls from the two security guys I knew on the team, and they were overjoyed to get their wired bonus money. They said it came at just the right time because they each had a payment that needed to be made and some of their pension money was still being held up for further review by the City of Philadelphia."

"I'm glad to hear this news, Chuck," Dave said, "now you go and buy something nice for Susan, OK?"

"Who's Susan?" Said Chuck and then added, "Just kidding. Actually, I think we are going to take a cruise to England on the Queen Mary 2. I might even get one of those fancy suites near the top deck, so I don't have to take a tuxedo for the formal dress nights. We can just order room service or go to the alternative dining room. She is talking about marriage, and I don't know how much longer I can hold out. If we do this thing in the fall, will you be my best man?"

"Of course," said Dave, "It would be a pleasure, just give me a month's notice, and I will be there."

"Gotta go now. Guess who is pulling into the driveway. Bye and thanks again, old friend."

"Take care, older friend," and Dave hung up before Chuck could answer back.

On Friday, April 14[th,] Dave arrived at Roger's office on Market Street in downtown Charlottesville just before 10 am. He was ushered into the conference room. About 10 minutes later, Roger and another man walked in, and Roger said, "Good morning, Dave. Meet Bruce Mathews, one of the principals in Davis and Mathews in Richmond. Dave shook hands with Bruce and exchanged pleasantries.

"Bruce, Dave was the project manager on the job to find Jefferson's DNA at the family cemetery near Monticello. He is a native of Charlottesville and had a career in project management with Comcast for 35 or so years, the last twenty of which was as Vice-President of Project Management. In addition, he holds a certification in project management from the Project Management Institute. I don't know how he does in public speaking, but that's your job. Bruce, why don't you outline for Dave some of the initial thoughts you have about our proposed press conference."

"Sure," said Bruce, "This and all press conferences should be carefully scripted with plenty of takeaways, meaning press packets of additional information and already answered questions. These packets allow us to limit the question period after the opening statement. The worst thing that can happen in a press conference is to let the Q&A get bogged down, and someone provides an off-the-cuff answer that blows up the conference."

"Understood, and I agree if you needed the support," said Dave.

Bruce continued, "I see the takeaway packet as having, at a minimum, copies of (1) the FBI analysis of the dental DNA sample, (2) the Affidavit from Dr. Patel saying the DNA samples were a match, (3) frequently asked questions, (4) a copy of the Jefferson letter to his sister Anna in late 1815 hinting about the relocation of their brother's remains, and finally (5) the DVD of the filming of the project starting with showing the cemetery survey and ending with the dental DNA sample being delivered to the FBI laboratory. I understand that the FBI doesn't allow any filming of the work in their facility, so we will have to trust that their reputation for independence and thorough analysis will stand up, at least in that area of FBI work. I heard from Roger that Dr. Bernstein also retrieved a second molar tooth next to the one sent to the FBI. Is that correct?"

"Yes, that is correct," said Dave.

"Good. I want to set up something that will have a great impact at the press conference. Roger tells me that Dr. Bernstein has that second sample still in its sealed package with evidence tape and his signature and a witness' signature going across the sealed opening. I want Dr. Bernstein to have that second sample in his coat pocket that day. We will script an answer for him to a press question centering on how do you know that these results are valid or is there any way to verify your results. I know several of the main players

198

here in town in TV and news, and they will be asking me what the press conference is all about to try to get advanced information. I might drop a hint about asking that kind of question or even set them up by saying we are worried about using up all the DNA samples to get our results; something like that happened with the 1998 DNA study, as I understand it. When that question comes up, the main speaker, which will be the property owner's representative, will turn to Dr. Bernstein to answer it. Dr. Bernstein will come up and take out the second sealed sample and say something to the effect that we anticipated this question, so we took a second tooth next to the first one using the same sealed evidence procedures; here is that second sample. And he will show the envelope with the evidence seal and signature to the audience so the TV guys can get a nice closeup of it. While doing that, he will say that it has been in his possession the entire time since both teeth were extracted in March. Then he will say that he is turning it over today to the attorney for the property owners for safekeeping until such time as a reputable second confirming analysis is needed or requested. And he will walk over to Roger and hand it to him and sit down. Quite an effect, don't you think?"

"Pretty good," said Dave. "Do you see a need for me to be there or to speak?"

"Oh, you definitely need to be there, and you may be needed to fill in some project details. We will give you a portfolio with some sample questions and proposed answers to study and have with you. It's OK to open it at the podium and get a glimpse of the answer as you get there before actually starting to speak. Everyone who might speak will have the same type of portfolio, so it will look professional and organized."

"Has a date been established, and where will this be done?"

"Roger and I think the best place is the Albemarle County office building, which is the old Lane High School facility. There is a nice auditorium in there to use for press conferences and a private way to get to the back of the auditorium, so we will bring everyone in the same limousine from Roger's office to the County office's side entrance. All of us will walk onto the stage together. One of my associates knows sign language, so she will sign for the entire press conference to make it look very official. Everyone will stand because that way, the conference can be cut off easier than if everyone is sitting on stage. As far as timing, we are thinking about 10 am on Wednesday, April 26th. That way, the TV folks have a splash for the noon news, and the news folks have time to look over their packets and write something for the next day's edition."

Bruce continued, "I should have a script for everyone within the next ten days, and we should schedule a meeting which is really a rehearsal in Roger's office for, say, Monday, April 24th. Is that date OK with you, Roger?"

Roger said, "It's fine with me. I know Jon Coolidge, the property owner's president, will be here that entire week because they have an annual meeting in May, and he wants to set up some things with the Omni Hotel before the date of that meeting. And Bruce, keep the announcement of the press conference from going out until you hear from me. We have to decide how and when to let the Foundation know about our results."

"OK, fine with me," said Bruce, "I will be back to you, Roger, with the scripts, and you can distribute them accordingly. Will you alert Dr. Bernstein to our plans, or do you want me to do that? We have done some work for Sol in the past, but it would be best coming from you."

"I will take care of bringing Sol up to speed," said Roger. "Dave, can you stay for a few minutes while I show Bruce out?"

"Sure, nice to meet you, Bruce, and I am sure the press conference will be well handled," said Dave.

"Nice to meet you also, Dave," said Bruce. "The one thing you can never discount is the press's ability to shoot you in the foot from left field, but we'll be as ready as we can be."

After showing Bruce out, Roger came back and said, "Bruce knows his stuff, so you don't have to worry about preparation, Dave. Jon wanted me to ask you to attend their annual meeting together with me as guests of the Association. That meeting will take place on Friday, May 5th at 10 am also at the Omni before they have their lunch. Are you available to join me there that morning? The members likely will have a number of questions. We'll show the DVD after Jon's opening remarks, and that will take up about an hour. Jon wants us to stay for lunch also. What do you think?"

Dave said, "I can certainly make the meeting and stay until the questions die down, but I feel a little queasy about staying for lunch. It is their organization, their property, and their lineage to Jefferson, and I would feel out of place."

"I feel the same way, so we can both make our exit before the lunch starts. By the way, after the big press conference, I was thinking about hosting a luncheon at Farmington for Bruce, Jon, you, and me. Are you interested in that?"

"That's very kind of you, Roger, but I might have other plans," said Dave, "I have a friend here who was part of the project; you may remember some wire transfers to a Richard Dunleavy. And there is another friend I want to invite to attend the press conference. So, we may go out to Boar's Head or even the Birdwood Golf Course grill. But thanks anyway. Are you going to discuss the Foundation notification with Jon?"

"Yes," said Roger, "I will be back to you in a couple of days about what he would like us to do."

"By the way, here is the key to the west gate at the graveyard," said Dave putting the key on Roger's desk.

As Dave drove home from the meeting in Roger's office, he thought to himself that this news would be electric in little ole Charlottesville, but he needed to take a vacation out of town afterward to clear his mind. He thought about calling Richard and then Lucy, telling them about the press conference, but he decided to wait a few days to make sure there wasn't a change in the dates or some other interruption.

Once he got home, his personal cell phone rang, but he didn't recognize the number, so he thought it best to let the voice message answer it. About a minute later, he heard the sound made when someone leaves a message, so he pushed the correct buttons to hear the message, which was,

"Mr. Hutchinson, this is Sam Carpenter of the *Daily Progress* again. I know you blocked calls from my other phones, but I wanted to speak with you about the work that was done at the Monticello graveyard. By the way, I am still waiting for an apology for how I was treated the one time I actually came to the job site. But I will forgive you if you call me back at this number. The public has a right to know what was done there, and I want to help you to tell that story."

That SOB is trying to shame me into calling him back, thought Dave, but it's not going to work. He then blocked future calls from that number. A week later, Roger Pettit called Dave on his personal cell phone number and said he had the press conference scripts now and asked Dave to stop by for his copy or he could have it delivered to his house. Dave said he needed to come by the County office

202

building the next day and then would stop in at Roger's office to get his script.

The next day, Dave stopped by the County office buildings to see the auditorium for himself and what back way there might be to enter that part of the building. Whatever way there might have been at one time, the office building was now locked up tightly in the back with only emergency escape doors. Security is now forcing people to go through the metal detectors at the main entrance on the west side as the only way into the building. There was a sign on each door that said "emergency exit only, not an entrance." He stopped by Roger's office to get his script and told Roger there was only one way into the building for public entrance. Roger said that Jon wanted the Foundation to be told about the results the Monday morning before the press conference but not be given data or a press package until Tuesday afternoon to avoid them analyzing it ahead of time and trying to pull a fast one at the press conference. Bruce would be given the go-ahead on the press conference notices to be released for Monday at lunch time.

Back home, Dave called Richard on his regular cell phone, having used up all of his burner phones. He got Richard's answering machine, so he left a message for Richard to call him when it was convenient. He then called Lucy, and she answered,

"Hello, Dave, keeping in touch?"

"Yes, and hi there, Lucy," Dave said, "There will be a press conference about the results of my project here in town on Wednesday, April 26th, and I was wondering if you would like to be here for that event."

"Wow, sounds like something amazing is going to happen, so yes, I would like to be there. What time does it start?"

"It starts at 10 am, but I wanted to see if you could get to my house about 9:20 that morning, and we would go to the conference then from here. Also, I wanted to see if you could stay for a while afterward and we would go out to lunch. If you need to see your mother instead, I would certainly understand."

"Why, Dave, that would be delightful to have lunch with you. I can see my mother another time. I have your address from last Christmas, so I can find my way there. I will be there promptly at 9:20 that morning. Are you the prime speaker?"

"No, just a backup when needed, which I hope won't often be," said Dave, "I will look forward to seeing you then. Bye."

The next day, Richard called and said he was working at the hospital when Dave had called. "What's up, brother?" Dave filled him in on the press conference details and hoped he could be there. Rich said he would certainly be there with bells on. And he thanked Dave for the bonus payment which had hit his bank account.

Then Dave said, "I have invited Lucy to come up for that event and to go to lunch afterward. I wanted you to join us for lunch also, and I was thinking about the Birdwood Golf Grill for a relaxed place to have a mini-celebration."

Rich said, "Sounds good to me, but you sure you want me to be the third wheel in this lunch?"

"Sure," said Dave, "You can even ask a lady friend to join us, but it's just lunch, and then you can go away, and maybe Lucy, and I will take a nice relaxing drive to the mountains if it's a nice day."

"Semper fi, brother, take care, see you on the 26th. Bye," said Richard.

Chapter Fifteen

Late April 2023

On April 24th, there was a rehearsal of the press conference team in Roger's office at 1 pm. Bruce Mathews, Jon Coolidge, Dr. Solomon Bernstein, Dave, and Roger were in the law office conference room. Bruce started the meeting by saying, "the press conference notice simply indicates that a press conference is being held to report on new DNA information on Thomas Jefferson as the possible father of one of Sally Hemings' children. In addition to all the local and state media, I expect that Fox and CNN from Washington would send camera crews and reporters. In essence, this press conference is going to be a *BIG* event with an emphasis on big. There likely will be follow-up one-on-one interviews required with the project participants. That will mean you should count on the afternoon being taken up with fifteen-to-twenty-minute increments of various interviews with Jon, Dr. Bernstein, and Dave. "

Dave wasn't happy with that announcement since he was hoping for some quality time with Lucy at long last. So, he asked, "Can some of that be done right after the press conference itself up until noon or 1 pm, rather than take up the entire afternoon."

"It can be," said Bruce, "but this news is going to be electric, and there will be a lot of requests for interviews."

"What about saying that we would be available by appointment on Thursday after they have read the materials in their packets?"

"Well, that works for print media, but TV will want interviews right away. Maybe I can set up six locations within the County office building, each one for a specific network camera crew, then rotating the three of you through each location for no more than fifteen minutes each for the TV guys. That should cover all the major networks. And I will take thirty-minute appointments for the print media for the next day. Roger, can we use your three conference rooms for that purpose again, to stage each of you in one conference room? I will rotate the print guys through starting at 10 am on Thursday. Like I said, guys, expect this announcement to be big news."

"That kind of schedule would work better for me," said Jon, "Because I have some Association business to attend around 3 pm on Wednesday." *Thank you, Jon,* thought Dave. Dr. Bernstein said it didn't matter to him, the school was over, and his schedule was free both Wednesday and Thursday because they were reading days before final exams. Roger said he wanted to take everyone to lunch on Wednesday at a private club and that he would make three conference rooms available to the group for all day on Thursday just to be safe.

"OK, that part is settled then," said Bruce, "Let's run through the scripts as a dress rehearsal for Wednesday."

Jon started out with his script as a welcome and introduction of the other people standing on the stage with him. He then outlined the reason the Association had decided to investigate the vacant area in the Southwest corner of the Jefferson graveyard. He continued with the role Dave played in the project to retrieve the dental DNA from a skull found in that area of the graveyard and his background. Next came the role that Dr. Bernstein played in the actual extraction and his background, along with the presence of a witness and the use of the FBI laboratory in Quantico, VA, for analysis of the tooth DNA. Next came the use of a board-certified pathologist, Dr. Patel, and his background, ultimately to compare the dental DNA of "patient XYZ" with the DNA of the descendant of Eston Hemings, the last son of Sally Hemings, whose DNA was the focus of the

Foster 1998 study. Jon then started to read the summary, but Bruce stopped him and said, "That took twelve minutes which is what we expected, now comes the summary and big bang."

Jon read the summary, which was "The identification of 'Patient XYZ,' whose male Y-chromosome DNA is identical to that of Eston Hemings, is Randolph Jefferson. Therefore, in conjunction with the professional opinion of Dr. Patel, the FBI analysis, and the procedures and results of a project to extract dental DNA from a grave site on our property, we believe at long last that science has identified the correct father of Eston Hemings as Randolph Jefferson, not Thomas Jefferson."

"Added to the audience gasps and possible reporters' live summation, that will take fifteen minutes," Bruce said. "Now, let's look at the possible questions and our suggested answers." The very first one was the suggested plant by Bruce earlier, having to do with a way to verify these conclusions or the possibility of more DNA sample material from Randolph Jefferson. Bruce said that would be Jon's cue to have Dr. Bernstein step up to the microphone and give the suggested answer involving the sealed second tooth that Sol would then turn over to Roger on the stage. Dave saw there were several questions about the project procedures and the suggested answers were bland and to the point without any embellishment which he said was fine with him and he would be prepared.

The dress rehearsal continued for another twenty minutes on "what ifs" and the prepared questions and answers. As they were leaving, Bruce said, "This may be the biggest thing to hit Charlottesville since the right-wing riots five years ago." *Let's hope no one dies this time,* Dave thought.

That afternoon, Roger called Dave on his personal cell phone and said,

"Jon and I had a discussion after our press conference rehearsal. He feels the Foundation should be told our results today before the press gets their announcement of the conference. I called Harrison on one phone while Jon called Clay Lawrence on another phone in our office. We both read off a script that included our delivery of a press packet to the Foundation by no later than 1 pm tomorrow, roughly a full day before the actual press conference. I don't think they will try to upstage us either before or at the press conference. We gave Bruce the go-ahead to send out the announcement of the conference at 5 pm tonight."

"Thanks for letting me know, Roger," said Dave, "And let's hope the Foundation is as forthright with us as we have been with them. I think they will wait to see the materials and hear what the reaction will be to the press conference."

Wednesday, April 26th, was a pretty spring morning in Charlottesville. It was sunny and 61 at 8 am that morning with an expected high of 72, but with a 50% threat of showers arriving between 3 and 4 pm. The dogwoods in town were in full bloom just in time for the Dogwood Festival completed over the past weekend.

Lucy arrived at Dave's house promptly at 9:20 am, and they both immediately got into Dave's car for the trip to the County office building. Dave didn't talk much on the drive to the press conference site, and Lucy sensed he was nervous, so she placed her hand on his right hand when it was not touching the wheel and said, "You will be great today, Dave Hutchinson, I'm confident this press conference will be great, and you will be great." That reassurance was just what Dave needed, and he relaxed some for the rest of the trip to the County office building.

The County building's parking lot was full near the office itself, and the TV vans with their antennae extended out were all lined up along the front curb on McIntire Road. It was a zoo, so Dave parked in one of the extra lots down on what used to be the Lane High football field. He and Lucy walked up to the west side entrance to the building and up the steps. Dave sensed that they were being filmed like attending a grand opening or the red-carpet walk. Once inside, they went through security and then went into the auditorium, which now served as the County Council meeting room. Dave found a nice aisle seat for Lucy about halfway back in the audience and told her to look out for Richard if she wanted to sit with someone she knew.

Dave then walked up the steps to the back of the stage to see Bruce standing there, but no Roger, Jon, or Dr. Bernstein. It was 9:50 am, but Bruce said that they were coming in a limousine together. Five minutes later, the three of them came up the steps to the stage and joined Bruce and Dave. Bruce's sign language lady was with them. Everyone had matching black portfolios with their scripts in them, plus any other notes. The auditorium was filling up rapidly, but the metal detecting screening was going slowly. All the TV cameras inside were lined up across the front on platforms to get them level with the stage. Dave thought this was a poor setup because some people in the audience would not be able to see the speaker's podium directly. He guessed that the TV folks ran the world when it came to press conferences. There were American flags on each side of the speaker's podium. Dave wondered if there would be a national anthem and prayer but suspected there would not be any of those things this time. At exactly 10:03 am, Bruce motioned for the group to walk onto the stage to their standing marks directly behind the speaker's podium. This was it, thought Dave.

Jon stepped up to the podium and microphone and said, "Good morning, ladies and gentlemen. My name is Jonathan Coolidge, and I am the current president of the Monticello Association, owner of the Jefferson family graveyard near Monticello. Joining me on stage this morning is Roger Pettit on my far left, who is legal counsel for the Association, Dr. Solomon Bernstein, next to Roger, who is the dean of the School of Dentistry at the Medical College of Virginia in Richmond, and to my right is David Hutchinson, a native of Charlottesville who was the lead project manager for the project I will be reporting on in a few minutes." Jon didn't introduce the lady signer, but she was standing just to the right of Jon and had already been working furiously.

Jon continued, "It has almost been 200 years since the death of Thomas Jefferson on July 4, 1826. For the last 25 years, there has been a great deal of history written and re-written about his relationship with a female enslaved person named Sally Hemings. There have been numerous books and articles written confirming or denying that Jefferson fathered one or more of the six children of Sally Hemings. In 1998, there was a DNA study done which scientifically confirmed that the last son of Sally Hemings, named Eston Hemings, was fathered by SOME JEFFERSON, but there was no scientific evidence establishing that it was specifically Thomas Jefferson who was the father. Yet, in spite of the lack of scientific proof, the study's author, Dr. Eugene Foster, stated that Jefferson was, in fact, the father. Later studies by the Thomas Jefferson Foundation gave great weight to oral histories of the enslaved families at Monticello and found notes written by Jefferson as to his presence at Monticello during loosely calculated conception dates for Sally Heming's six children. The Foundation concluded that it was likely that Thomas Jefferson was the father of Eston Hemings, and there was a high probability that he fathered all six of the children of Sally Hemings. In 2018, the Foundation chose to eliminate those qualifying words from its conclusion and revised its website to show that, without a doubt, Thomas Jefferson fathered all six of the children of Sally Hemings."

"The Monticello Association membership is made up of lineal descendants of Thomas and Martha Jefferson. Last year around this time, we decided to initiate and fund a project to retrieve dental DNA from a suspected unmarked grave on our property without having to exhume the skeletal remains, something we have resisted doing even after dental DNA has become a standardized procedure as a rich source of DNA material. Our project was ably managed by David Hutchinson, a Charlottesville native and certified project manager with 38 years of experience with Comcast, most recently as Vice President of Project Management until his retirement two years ago. Dave first engaged a ground-penetrating radar company with cemetery-specific software and experience to survey a 600-square-foot section of the Southwest corner of the original Jefferson graveyard. That survey disclosed that there was, indeed, a burial there without a marker and a skull, and some large bones remained. There were some other findings as well, but this skull was the focus of the project thereafter. Dave's team then used normal Ditch Witch horizontal drilling equipment, similar to that used to install fiber optic cables underground, along with ground penetrating radar to access the grave site with an opening directly above the right jaw of the buried skull. Then, Dr. Solomon Bernstein, dean of the Dental School at the Medical College of Virginia, directed the final access to the teeth area and extracted a molar tooth for dental DNA material using custom dental equipment controlled remotely from about twenty feet away. An independent witness observed the tooth extraction, and both he and Dr. Bernstein signed the evidence tape and sealed the tooth in an evidence pouch. They both then personally delivered the dental DNA sample, known anonymously as "Patient XYZ," to the FBI DNA laboratory in Quantico, VA. This FBI laboratory is a noted expert in the DNA identification field and was engaged for analysis and description of the molecular DNA chemistry of that DNA sample, including genetic sequences."

"Once the FBI analysis and genetic sequence had been received, we arranged for Dr. Sanjay Patel, board-certified pathologist and chief of the pathology department at the University of Virginia

Hospital, to compare the DNA haplotype sequences of 'Patient XYZ' with the DNA haplotype sequences of the descendant of Eston Hemings, whose DNA was used in the 1998 Foster study. His report to us stated that, in his professional opinion, the two DNA fingerprints were identical, which indicated a 99.9% probability that 'Patient XYZ' and Eston Hemings were directly related in a linear family. We are reporting today that conclusive scientific evidence now exists that 'Patient XYZ' is Randolph Jefferson and that he was the father of Eston Hemings, not Thomas Jefferson."

The crowd noise was spontaneous, with gasps, wows, groans, and shouts like the Genie bottle had exploded. Bruce came onto the stage, and Jon stepped back from the podium. Bruce said, "Ladies and gentlemen, let's everyone calm down and continue with the press conference. For the press, there are packets of information as you leave containing copies of the FBI analysis, the professional opinion of Dr. Patel, other documents, and a DVD of the entire project from the time of starting the first cemetery survey activity to delivering the dental DNA sample to the FBI. We have time only a few questions right now. Step up to the microphone in the center aisle and state your name and affiliation." Bruce stepped back from the podium and pointed to the first guy standing at the center microphone,

"Chad Thomas with the *Richmond Times Dispatch*. Mr. Coolidge, are you confident that this dental DNA is legitimate? I mean, how will anyone else know or confirm your group's results?" Dave couldn't believe it; the very first question was the one Bruce had planted.

Jon said, "I would like Dr. Bernstein to answer that question." Dr. Bernstein stepped up to the microphone and delivered his pre-arranged answer together with the handoff of the second tooth to

Roger. You could almost see the jaw drop of the questioner and other people in the audience. The next person stepped up and said,

"Sarah Goodrich, Fox News, Washington. Mr. Coolidge, what do you expect the reaction to be to your project's results from the Thomas Jefferson Foundation and the Hemings family descendants?" This was a question Bruce had put on the dress rehearsal schedule as a possibility.

Jon said, "Our goal for this project simply was to follow the truth wherever it led, just as Thomas Jefferson said in his letter to William Roscoe on December 27, 1820, in describing his new University of Virginia. I cannot answer for any other party outside of our membership as to what the impact may be on this new scientific data. Reasonable people differ on many things, but we welcome any worthy science-based analysis of our work, and as you have just seen, there is a way to the confirmation of our results in the event an organization wants to do so. I will add that the Foundation was apprised of our project at the very beginning, and we received their full cooperation throughout this project." The next guy looked familiar to Dave, but he couldn't come up with a name until,

"Sam Carpenter, *Charlottesville Daily Progress*. My question is for Mr. Hutchinson." Dave stepped up to the podium, "Why was the project done under such tight security and a news blackout? I went to the work site and was treated with rudeness and physical abuse just because I was a part of the press trying to do my job and keep the public informed." So, you finally have your interview, Mr. Carpenter, Dave thought. He had actually thought about a similar question, so he was ready to send a message back.

"Mr. Carpenter," Dave said, "The project was conducted under the direction of the property owner's desire to keep it secret until a dental DNA source was actually extracted and properly examined. This project was not a Facebook report where actions are posted on a continuum of constant updates. This project had a defined goal that, if reached, would then be newsworthy, but not before or during it. A newspaper friend of mine said once that 'some news is not fit to print,' and I have always remembered that. As to your last assertion about rude and physical mistreatment, we had trained security guards there day and night to protect the property owner's right to privacy as to what was happening inside the graveyard. We also have you on camera from both the body cameras of the two security persons talking to you that day and another tree-mounted camera. If you want to pursue some legal remedy on this matter, we will see you in court. In the meantime, you were treated the same way that all visitors to Jefferson's graveyard were treated, Mr. Carpenter, with courtesy and respect," said Dave, with his voice rising slightly at the end. You could almost see Carpenter slink away.

Bruce stepped up to the microphone and said, "That's all the time we have for questions right now, but the principals will be in various interview rooms here in the County offices for any further questions or interviews by the TV news only under strict fifteen-minute maximum guidelines. For the TV press, your packets will be available at the back of the auditorium and will have those room locations for you to set up your equipment, and then each of the principals will rotate around to your room. For the print press, the three principals will be available tomorrow morning in Roger Pettit's office for pre-scheduled thirty-minute interviews. There are forms in your press kits to fill out for an interview at a time to be confirmed with you later today. Thank you all for attending this press conference."

Dave's 75 total minutes of six interviews were a blur, and he was anxious to get out of there. Back in the auditorium, which was now mostly empty, he saw Lucy sitting with Richard. As Dave approached, the two of them stood up, and Lucy said,

214

"Way to take down that young pest today, Dave; great answer. That's the problem with the press today, they get all their news from Twitter and think the public is entitled to know everything all the time, like on Facebook. Hey, you even remembered the breakout session title. Good for you."

Richard said, "Lucy and I have been reviewing all the things you did in high school, those she knew about and those I knew about, so all your dirty laundry is hanging out there now, brother."

"Thanks for small favors, old friend," said Dave, "But I am really ready for lunch in a quiet place. I've got more of these interviews tomorrow, but I want to escape for the rest of the day somewhere nice with nice people. Are you and a lady friend joining us?"

"Well, actually, no. I need to head to Richmond now. My VA appointment was moved up from tomorrow to this afternoon at 3 pm, so I need to get on the road. So, you two behave yourselves, and I will see you again, Lucy, soon I hope."

"Take care, Richard," said Lucy. "And thanks for keeping me company while the big guy took center stage." Rich left the auditorium.

As they walked to their car, Dave said, "What would you like to do for lunch?"

Lucy said, "I know a nice quiet place if you have sandwich stuff at your house."

"I don't have much in the way of lunch stuff. I eat lunch out most of the time," replied Dave. "But we can stop at the Bellair Market right at the entrance to my neighborhood and get a great sandwich there to take back to the house."

"Fine with me, sounds good," Lucy said.

They looked over the sandwich menu on the ordering kiosk at Bellair Market. Dave got a Farmington sandwich, and Lucy got an Ednam. They also got a bag of chips and two cookies and drove to Dave's house. As they were getting out of his car, Lucy stopped at her car and opened the passenger side door. She took out a small bag, and to keep Dave from asking about it, she said, "This is my satchel of necessities."

"What's in your satchel of necessities?" Dave said as he opened the front door.

"Well, there are some replacement parts for my wooden leg, a second glass eye in case the first one falls out, another wig if I should need it, and a bag of peanut M&M's. I never go anywhere without them." She put the bag down by the couch, and they walked back to the kitchen area. "You have a nice eye for color, Dave," said Lucy, "and I see a lot of framed golf pictures."

"Yes," said Dave, "I have gotten several limited-edition prints of famous golf holes in this country done by Linda Hartaugh, the noted golf course painter. There are two from Augusta National and one from Pine Valley. What would you like to drink?"

"Water will be fine for me." And they sat down on the porch with their sandwiches and drink and watched the clouds rolling in for some possible rain later. After lunch was finished and the trash was thrown away, Lucy said,

"Do I get the fifty cents tour of the rest of your house?"

"Sure," said Dave, and he led her to the man cave appointed as an office and then to the guest bedroom. "Well, that's about it."

"What about your bedroom? Is there an extra fee for that?"

"No, but my bed is not made," Dave said sheepishly.

"I didn't expect it would be. Men are not interested in a tidy bedroom."

As they stepped into Dave's bedroom, Lucy leaned over against Dave and said, "I think it's time for our snoring reduction experiment."

Dave went over to the window, pulled the lined drapes closed, and said, "These really help make it dark. I want to warn you that there is only one rule to this experiment," as he walked back over to Lucy, who was still by the door.

"What's that?" Lucy whispered.

"You can't leave right after the experiment is finished."

"That's why I have a satchel of necessities," Lucy said, looking up at Dave and smiling.

Dave kissed her as he closed the door to the bedroom, reducing the light to a minimum, and the first roll of distant thunder was heard.